The Decker brothers were getting off the train when two big men with glowering looks approached them. Now Cal and Hale were in for it for having taught the conductor a lesson or two about good manners. One of the men stood before Cal rubbing his knuckles in a meaty hand.

"Put hands on him, didn't he?" he demanded.

"I guess you can call it that," Cal conceded. "But your conductor refused to answer a civil question."

Bill flashed a triumphant glance at his companion. "You heard that, Dan? Looks like Abe reported it right."

Dan nodded heavy approval. "Looks to me like they could stand a little mannering."

"Is it the railroad's policy to manner its customers, or your own idea?" Cal purred.

It took Bill and Dan a moment for that to sink into their heads, then their faces slowly turned red.

"Why, goddamn you," Bill roared and lumbered forward.

Cal heard Hale's yelp of delight, but had no time to notice how Hale was doing. His full attention was centered on the man before him. He had bulk on his hands, a slow bulk, but Cal didn't know how tough he was. There was only one way to find out—dive in and get wet.

Other ACE Books by Giles A. Lutz:

A TIME FOR VENGEANCE
THE BLIND TRAIL
THE CHALLENGER
DEADLY LIKE A .45
DEMANDING LAND
GUN RICH
THE HONYOCKER
LAW OF THE TRIGGER
MAN ON THE RUN
MY BROTHER'S KEEPER
NEMESIS OF CIRCLE A
REPRISAL!
STAGECOACH TO HELL
THE STRANGER
THE TROUBLE BORROWER
THE VENGEANCE GHOST
WILD RUNS THE RIVER

THE RAGGED EDGE

by

Giles A. Lutz

ace books
A Division of Charter Communications Inc.
A GROSSET & DUNLAP COMPANY
360 Park Avenue South
New York, New York 10010

THE RAGGED EDGE

Copyright © 1978 by Giles A. Lutz

All rights reserved. No part of this book may be reproduced in any form or by any means, except for the inclusion of brief quotations in a review, without permission in writing from the publisher.

All characters in this book are fictitious. Any resemblance to actual persons, living or dead, is purely coincidental.

An ACE Original

First ACE printing: August, 1978

Published simultaneously in Canada

Printed in U.S.A.

Chapter One

CAL DECKER STARED out of the train window again. Was the damned train actually slowing down, or was that just wistful hoping? He flattened his nose against the glass, but that didn't increase his range of vision. If there was a town somewhere ahead, he couldn't see a sign of it.

"Have to be right in the middle of the damn town, before I can see it," he muttered.

Cal's brother sat across from him on the hard bench, his eyes vacant with boredom. It had been a long and grinding trip from Texas to South Dakota, and Hale Decker had been squirming uncomfortably the last two days.

"Just talking to myself," Cal explained. "That's the only way I can find a level of intelligence I can appreciate." Cal grinned in anticipation. That should bring Hale up off his bench, howling with indignation. Instead, Hale's chin sank lower on his chest, and his eyes closed.

Cal shook his head in sympathy. Not being able to get a spark of response from Hale proved to Cal how much this trip had taken out of his brother. Cal didn't approve of Hale getting this low, but he could understand. Hale had been sulky and morose when they entrained in Texas, and each passing mile deepened his black mood.

Cal knew he was getting a little tight himself. He almost yelled at Hale, cutting off the hot words just in time. He didn't like leaving Texas any better than Hale did. He had spent more than half of the journey arguing with Hale, trying to point out why this move was necessary. He hadn't even come close to changing Hale's mind. His brother had a stubborn streak in him a mile wide. Once Hale got his mind set on something, dynamite couldn't blast it out.

Cal shrugged and looked out the window again. Well, the old man could argue with his youngest son when he got here. Cal was sick of this useless, never ending bickering with Hale.

Cal shifted his weight, trying to find a spot on his butt that was better padded. The unrelenting hardness of the seats on this train had worn his butt thin. This goddamned train had only two speeds; slow and slower, and this had to be the latter one. Dammit, Cal could get off and walk faster than this train was moving.

Meyers, the conductor, a short, pudgy man with a tired unhappy face, came into the car. Cal hadn't liked the man almost from the first moment he saw him. Meyers was officious and brusque of manner, and his curtness rubbed Cal raw. Getting information out of him was like trying to wring water out of a granite rock. Maybe the man wasn't pleased with his job, Cal thought, or maybe he had a miserable home life. However, Cal didn't give a damn what the reason was for the churlishness. He and Hale were paying customers on this damned railroad, and Cal expected just common, ordinary courtesy.

Hale beat Cal to the question he was just going

to ask. "Hey, Meyers, when do we get to Evarts?"

The conductor looked as though the question was outrageous. His face turned mean and he bit off his words. "You'll know that when we get there!"

Cal sucked in a hard breath. Meyers, must have thought that uniform placed him above everyone else and gave him license to say what he pleased. Cal's muscles bunched. He had put up with this for too long. It was time to teach Meyers a lesson in controlling his tongue.

The same impulse was exploding in Hale's mind. He was on his feet before Cal could straighten up. Hale reached Meyers in two long strides and clamped a hand on his shoulder. Cal knew that raw, savage look all too well. It said that Meyers' rudeness had ripped off the lid of Hale's volatile temper.

Cal couldn't reach Hale before he laid violent hands on Meyers, but he might be able to prevent the punishment Hale intended handing out to the conductor.

Hale's face was savage as he swung Meyers around. "Why, you little horse turd," he roared. "When I ask you a question, I expect a civilized answer." He seized Meyers by both shoulders and shook him viciously.

Cal, catching just a glimpse of Meyers' bugging eyes and slack mouth as Hale's violent shaking made a blur of Meyers' face, grabbed one of Hale's wrists. His muscles bulged as his fingers bit deep.

"That's enough," he said quietly. He locked eyes with Hale. For a moment, Cal was certain his brother had enough fury left to spill over on him, and he knew it wouldn't be the first time. "You hear me, Hale?" Cal snapped.

Sanity began to filter back into Hale's eyes—maybe due to the memory of all those other encounters between them, or maybe from the habit of listening to his older brother all these years.

The red left Hale's eyes. He looked a little embarrassed as he said, "Aw, Cal. He got to me. I'm so tired of taking his lip."

Cal nodded and murmured, "Yeah." He understood. His voice was easy, though the ring of authority was still there. He had four years on Hale and maybe twenty pounds. For quite a few years Hale had looked up to him for direction. Habit becomes a strong chain, but maturity had a way of weakening such a chain and Cal had seen its weakening coming for a long time.

Hale still hadn't let go of Meyers. He put his face close to the conductor's and said softly, "I asked you a question, Meyers."

There was a touch of green in Meyers' face, and his lips were slack. He gulped a few times to quiet his jerky breathing, but he still couldn't meet the glare in Hale's eyes.

He looked away as he muttered, "We should be pulling into Evarts in the next fifteen minutes."

Meyers then dared a glance at Hale. His tongue may have been taught some manners, but his eyes hadn't learned a thing. They were still filled with spite.

Cal knew Hale saw that spite and he saw the flush tightening along Hale's jaw line. Maybe Cal had let go of Hale too soon. The cords in Hale's forearms stood out like small cables. Cal was afraid Hale was going to slam Meyers into the car's wall.

"Hale," he warned. "You got what you wanted out of him."

Hale's laugh was forced, but it was an attempt at lightness. "You could be right, Cal." He shoved Meyers from him but not as forcefully as Cal had feared. Hale's rage had obviously lessened. He didn't smash Meyers into the wall, and he caught his balance after a single, unsteady step.

Meyers' lips were a thin, ugly line. His complexion was a mottled red and white; the color of an angry man.

Cal's eyes bored into Meyers. Don't be a damned fool, he thought. Let it drop right here.

Meyers' eyes flickered from face to face. He licked his lips, and Cal could almost see him making up his mind. Meyers suddenly whirled and proceeded him down the aisle. His haste was driven by rage. It made him look ludicrous, but Cal didn't feel like laughing. He was relieved that Meyers had enough sense not to push harder against Hale's temper.

Meyers marched to the car door before he turned. His face was malevolent, but he had been wise enough to put that much distance between himself and Hale.

"You damned cowboys," he said shrilly. "You think you own the whole damned world. You ain't heard the end of this yet. I'll show—" He was so mad he was spluttering and paused to catch a fresh breath. "By God, I'm telling you—"

"You turd!" Hale yelled and took a step toward Meyers.

Alarm washed Meyers' face. He whirled and

scurried out of the car.

Cal was afraid Hale would dash after Meyers and was ready to grab his brother. Then he saw that Hale was laughing in deep-seated belly roars. He ended his burst of mirth by chuckling, "I guess this means he'll report us to the railroad."

"Probably," Cal said flatly. He wasn't worried about that, for no matter how much Meyers exaggerated the incident, Cal didn't think the railroad would do anything drastic about Meyers' report. What could they do, he asked. The cowboys that Meyers so scorned were going to bring the railroad a hell of a lot of money.

But Cal was worried how the old man would take this, if he heard about the ruckus. Cal was too accustomed to Pardee's wrath whenever he thought his dignity had been affronted. Their father could pour out more hell on his two sons than the railroad could ever imagine.

Cal's sober mien got through to Hale, because he asked, "Don't tell me you're worried about what that fat little man could say?"

"Not him," Cal answered. "But the old man won't be happy, if he hears about it. We're coming to a new country, and you know how touchy Pardee can be. He doesn't want a black mark on the Decker name."

Hale tried to shrug the words away, but he couldn't hide the flicker of unease in his eyes. How very well he knew what Cal was talking about.

Cal wanted to lecture Hale about why they were here, but Hale knew all that. Repeating it once more, or a dozen times, wouldn't drive it into Hale's head if it wasn't already there.

He sighed as he saw the return of that sulky set

on Hale's face. Hale was only twenty years old and he had a lot of growing up to do. Not in a physical way, for Hale was a mature man. No, it was his mental processes that needed maturing.

Cal stared at his brother a moment longer. A strong family resemblance was there. Cal was the taller by a good two inches, but both of them had that same lean, hard cut to the jaw. Cal had a calmness that showed in the relaxed easy way he looked at a man. Hale was like a pot too filled and constantly bubbling, threatening to spill over at the slightest nudge. He did things with greater intensity than Cal, in his play, in his work, and in his fighting. He puts out a hell of a lot more energy, but his results are a little on the skinny side, Cal reflected.

Losing their mother two years ago had been a terrible blow to the both of them. Cal had hidden his grief well, but Hale had gone completely to pieces. He had raised more pure hell in the following few months than Cal had raised in all of his life. Cal had gotten Hale out of jail too many times, usually for drunk and disorderly conduct. Losing Sarah had cut all Hale's anchoring strings. For a while there, Cal was sure Hale would never be able to beat his way back to stable ground. And he thought Pardee would choke on his rage before Hale returned to normal. Still, Cal wasn't completely convinced the wildness was over. It continued to flicker occasionally in Hale's eyes, though nothing serious now happened. The lull in Hale's erratic behavior reminded Cal of lightning striking through a dark summer sky. It promised violence, but nobody could predict if or where it could hit.

Cal pushed those thoughts aside. Losing Sarah had been a bad time for all three of them. Pardee never talked about his wife's death; he just grew older and grimmer. Sarah's death was the start of the circumstances that drove the Deckers out of Texas—that and the drought that started right after Sarah died and deepened the following year. People said, "It'll rain. Hell, it always has." Each passing month only proved what god-awful liars those people were. Pardee wasn't a giving-in man, but he was smart enough to get out of Texas while he still had something to take with him.

The sulkiness on Hale's face irritated Cal, and he almost snapped at him. Dammit, Hale wasn't the only one suffering. This move was grinding all of them fine.

Instead, Cal put a hard hand on his bothersome thoughts and said mildly, "Better get our things together, Hale." He guessed he had a little of that wild lightning in him too, for it flickered briefly— Don't you argue with me now, Hale, he thought, or I'll pound your damned head off.

For a moment tension flared between them. Cal would almost have welcomed a clash as a physical outlet for the churning forces within him. Instead he turned away abruptly. Trouble was the easiest thing a man could find. Avoiding it was the difficult part, and a man rarely got credit for that.

Cal lifted his leather chaps off the hook and laid them on the bench. He bent over, pulled his warbag out into the aisle, and checked its contents to be sure he hadn't forgotten anything. His pants were drawn tight over his butt.

He didn't actually hear Hale move, but some instinct warned him and he looked over his shoulder. Hale, holding his own chaps, swung them hard. Cal didn't have time to straighten before the leather whacked him across the butt. Leather swung like this had a powerful force—the chaps stung like hell as they landed.

Cal expelled a tearing breath as he jerked erect, his hurt and rage turning everything red before him.

"Why, damn you!" he roared, whirling on Hale. If this was what Hale wanted, it suited Cal just fine.

But Cal couldn't believe his eyes. Hale's grin was plastered all over his face, and he backed away, holding the chaps in one hand, the other held placatingly before him. Laughter was choking his words, making them almost unintelligible.

"That's for that smart-ass remark about my level of intelligence," Hale gasped.

The belligerence leaked out of Cal, taking the anger off his face. Hale wasn't trying to push animosity into an open fight. This was his idea of a joke. And at the same time, he gets back at me, Cal thought.

Cal rubbed his stinging butt. Hale was right; it had been a smart-ass remark. Cal grinned reluctantly. That damned Hale had a quick and facile mind. He paid me back without pushing it into an open brawl between us.

Hale had been watching his brother warily, not certain how Cal would take this. He was relieved to see Cal grin.

"Your round," Cal conceded. "I'll file it away and get around to paying it off one of these days."

Hale could double over with his laughter now in full abandon. "I couldn't help it, Cal. You made such a beautiful target."

The stinging was fading, and Cal's grin was true.

"I guess I did," he said ruefully. He looked around as he became aware that the motion of the train had stopped. "Hey, we must be at Evarts." He picked up his warbag and chaps. "You go ahead of me. I want to keep an eye on you."

Hale wiped his eyes and picked up his gear. "Thought you would," he said and chuckled.

Hale was the first one to start down the car's steps. He paused at the bottom and looked back at Cal. "Looks like we got a welcoming committee."

Cal frowned. That was odd. They didn't know any one in Evarts. Who would form a welcoming committee? He pushed Hale to the ground and stepped down beside him.

He started looking around, and Hale said, "Over to your right."

Cal turned his head in that direction. Meyers and two burly men were coming their way. Their purpose was clear in the set scowls on their faces. Railroad men, Cal thought. Maybe the brakeman and a switchman. Meyers stayed a careful step behind them, his face alight with malicious satisfaction.

"Meyers didn't wait long to make his report," Cal said casually and dropped his warbag and chaps to the ground. He liked the savage grin flashing across Hale's face. The old family solidarity was back between them.

"Wouldn't be very neighborly not to listen to what they want to say, would it?" Hale asked softly.

"Not in the least," Cal assured him. Maybe Pardee wouldn't like a brawl the first minute of their arrival, but dammit Pardee had never taught them to run, had he?

Chapter Two

CAL MADE HIS appraisal as the three approached. Meyers carefully made no effort to catch up with the other two, and Cal knew he could count him out entirely. Meyers wasn't here for any part in the physical action that might take place. He was here only for satisfaction.

The other two were an entirely different matter. Both of them were big, outweighing Cal and Hale, though Cal would say they had a soft edge about them. Instead of being in uniform their clothes were greasy and work worn. Slow too, he decided as he watched them approach. But there was an unmistakable stamp of purpose in their faces. Those glowering looks said they had some kind of a grievance they intended to put straight. Meyers must have embellished his report to them.

Cal glanced at Hale. While his face was blank, there was a light shining out of his eyes. Hale welcomed whatever was ahead. Maybe that was just my imagination, Cal thought. But he had seen that shining light before. Hale liked trouble, and if it was already brewing, what was so wrong about giving it a little stir?

Neither Cal nor Hale said a word. They didn't have to; they read each other perfectly. Each took a sideways step, widening the gap between them. The two big men would have to separate to get at them. That lessened the chances of both men jumping together on Cal or Hale. It also reduced the chances of either Cal or Hale taking a concentrated battering in those first few seconds. The odds weren't bad at all. It would be only one on one.

The big men stopped about four feet from Cal and Hale, their faces still grim.

"These the two, Abe?" the man in front of Cal asked.

Cal made a quick evaluation of the two and their rating went down another notch. These were mouthy men, men who chose talk before action. Cal never found this kind particularly dangerous. The ones he worried about were those who did what was on their minds without preliminaries.

"That's them, Bill." Meyers' voice was shrill and vindictive. "The smaller one manhandled me."

Meyers' description almost brought a grin to Cal's lips. How Hale would resent that. So Abe was Meyers' first name.

Cal checked Hale's impatient forward surge. "The conductor's got that wrong," Cal said mildly. "He wasn't manhandled." He knew, of course, Hale had shaken Meyers a little, but it depended upon which viewpoint the observer took.

Bill reflectively rubbed his knuckles in a meaty hand. "Put hands on him, didn't he?" he demanded.

"I guess you can call it that," Cal conceded. "But your conductor refused to answer a civil question."

Bill flashed a triumphant glance at his companion. "You heard that, Dan? Looks like Abe reported it right."

Dan nodded heavy approval. "Looks to me like they could stand a little mannering."

"Is it the railroad's policy to manner its customers, or your own idea?" Cal purred.

It took Bill and Dan a moment for that to sink into their heads, and their faces slowly turned red.

"Why, goddamn you," Bill roared and lumbered forward.

Cal heard Hale's yelp of delight, but had not time to notice how Hale was doing. His full attention was centered on the man before him. He had bulk on his hands, a slow bulk, but Cal didn't know how tough he was. There was only one way to find out—dive in and get wet.

Cal glided forward, watching those heavy fists. His sudden attack momentarily loosened Bill's mouth and filled his eyes with alarm. He threw his blow before Cal was fully within range. Cal jerked his head to one side and let the fist slide over his shoulder. He dug a fist deep into that massive belly, and the rush of breath from Bill's mouth told him it was a good blow. The pallor of Bill's face and the sickness in his eyes confirmed it.

Pardee had always told Cal that if a fight was necessary, be sure he got in the first lick. That first lick could be worth as much as seventy-five percent of the fight.

Cal didn't take time to add up his percentages. His fists pummeled away like blades of a windmill gone berserk, cruelly punishing the big man. Bill might not have known it, but he had lost the fight with that first blow. But he was tough, though unskilled. He flailed away, and one of those glancing blows tried to rip off Cal's ear.

Cal shook his head to ease the ringing in his ear and drew a fresh breath. The force of that blow told him what could happen to him if he blundered into another one. He didn't know how Hale was doing and right now had no time to do any checking. He could hear the scuffling of feet and the grunts and oaths. Dan was a profane fighter, spewing obscenities upon Hale. That would probably cost him in the long run. Hale would see to that.

Cal beat Bill back a step at a time, knowing a fierce and primitive satisfaction each time his fists landed. Bill was beginning to hurt bad. His breathing came in great, slobbering gasps, and each exhalation spewed out a spray of bloody moisture. He hawked frequently to clear his throat, then rid himself of the bloody mass in his mouth. He knew he was losing; it showed in the deep, agonized lines in his face, and in the way his fists kept sinking lower and lower, despite his efforts to hold them up. But he never quit. Cal could give him full credit for that.

Cal kept hoping Bill would blurt out he'd had enough, but some stubborn inclination wouldn't let the words come out. Cal was hurting too, but in a different way. His lungs labored, and he felt the deadly lethargy crawling up his legs, turning them into heavy weights he had to drag around. This couldn't last more than a minute or two, before this kind of exertion took it all out of him.

He knocked aside Bill's feeble defense and smashed him full on the point of the chin. Cal almost yelped with the solid mass of pain that started in his knuckles, then ran the length of his arm. He gave Bill more credit. Dammit he thought in disgust. He could have a broken hand bone on that hard-headed bastard.

Bill's head rocked back, but he didn't go down. His eyes were wide with shock, and looked as though he no longer had the power to close his mouth.

Maybe Bill deserved the right to have this finished in a way that wouldn't rip his pride. Cal hit him with the left fist, trying to duplicate the other blow. The blow didn't miss by more than a fraction of an inch.

Cal stared at his opponent in awe. Bill's head flopped around as though his neck was broken, but he was still on his feet. What was it going to take to knock Bill off his feet? Cal gritted his teeth. Hitting a defenseless man wasn't the most pleasant thing in the world, but Bill seemed to want it that way.

Cal reached back and gathered all the remaining strength he had in his left arm. He hit Bill's chin again, and the sodden splat of the landing blow made an ugly sound.

Bill stayed on his feet, his eyes vacant, his breathing a nasty, tearing sound. Dammit, Cal swore again. That wasn't enough to finish him. He was going to have to hit him again, and Cal doubted he had enough strength left for a good solid blow. Then he saw the slow buckling of Bill's knees. He wavered back and forth, instinctively trying to retain his balance, then he leaned forward, picking up more momentum with each inch of his fall.

Bill fell like a great tree which had been deeply undercut, gaining more speed until he crashed against the ground. He bounced from the impact, but there was no conscious reflex left in him.

Cal knew Bill wouldn't get up, not for a time anyway. He gulped in great draughts of air to ease the fire in his lungs and repeatedly shook his head to clear away the little black spots dancing before his eyes. He unconsciously rubbed his aching fist as he stared at the inanimate bulk. He felt no anger, no resentment, only a great weariness. He would have given anything just to be able to sit down.

Cal raised his head, to see Meyers staring at him. Temper started building up in Cal again. None of this had been necessary, but a petty, little satisfaction had made its demands.

Meyers looked at the prone figure, then back at Cal. He looked as though he couldn't believe what he saw. His face was a pasty white and his lips trembled. He read some menace in Cal's manner and squalled, "Don't you touch me." He backpedalled hastily, trying to put distance between himself and Cal.

The ludricrousness of his flight brought a faint grin to Cal's lips. Meyers was safe, if he only knew it. Cal didn't have enough strength to chase him a half-dozen feet.

A string of oaths jerked Cal back to reality. Hell, he had forgotten all about Hale's part in this. He jerked his head around in time to see Hale going down from a blow in the face. It must have stunned him, for he didn't try to get up, and his face was empty.

Dan yelled with pleasure and charged him. He pulled up a stride short of Hale and swung his leg to get full power behind it. His kick caught Hale in the ribs, the force of it thudding as Hale's body hit the ground.

Cal wasn't nearly as weary as he thought he was. "Why you sonuvabitch," he yelled as he ran at Dan.

Dan had his leg drawn back for another kick, and Cal saw that he wasn't going to reach him in time to knock the thought of another kick out of his head. Cal did the only thing that was left open to him. He left his feet in a dive, his shoulder catching Dan just above the knee of the leg he stood on.

Dan squalled as the knee buckled, spilling him onto his face. The impact of Cal's body and the fall put a severe wrench on Dan's knee. He rolled over and sat up, groaning as he grabbed his aching joint.

Cal, planted before Dan, forgot that his fist was aching and he cocked it high. "You sonuvabitch," he repeated, his rage running the words together. "Get up and try kicking me."

He stared at that bloodied face. Hale had done some damage before Dan's last blow knocked him down. Cal ached for Dan to get up. He wanted to draw some more blood from that battered face.

"Come on, get up," he taunted.

Dan rocked back and forth, still holding the knee. "I can't. I'm hurt real bad."

"Remind me to cry about that after this is over," Cal reached a hand toward Dan. "You'll get up, or I'll jerk you to your feet."

"No, you won't," Hale interrupted.

Cal glanced at his brother. Hale was sitting up, and if his eyes weren't perfectly clear, they were clearing rapidly.

Hale shook his head and blinked his eyes. "You always were a hog when it came to fun. That one belongs to me."

Cal grinned in open relief. That was all the proof he needed to tell him that Hale was all right.

Just the same he watched Hale closely as he scrambled to his feet. That could have been a wince on Hale's face, and Cal had the impression that Hale momentarily clutched at the spot where the kick had landed. But Hale moved easily enough after that, and Cal thought he could put all his misgivings down to a fearful imagination.

Hale walked over and planted himself before Dan. "Get up, you son-of-a-bitch," he said softly. "You asked for this."

Dan still held his knee. "I can't," he protested again. "I twisted my knee."

"Remind me later I owe you sympathy," Hale jeered. His hand flicked out and slapped Dan smartly across the face.

Dan's head rocked under the blow, and his eyes were wide and startled. The outline of Hale's palm stood out in stark relief before the blood started rushing back.

Dan's eyes watered, and he bleated, "Here now. You can't do that."

"Stop me," Hale said coldly. "I owe you something for that kick. I'm going to collect one way or another. I can stand here and slap your face to a pulp, if that's the way you want it."

Dan stared at that unforgiving face, blinking to keep back tears of frustration. "It's a hell of a thing," he said plaintively, "not to give a hurt man any more chance than this."

That seemed to drive Hale wild. "Why, damn you," he said passionately. "You've earned what you've got coming and now you try to talk your way out of it. One way or the other, Mister, you're going to pay your dues." He slapped Dan with the other hand, and the white outline briefly appeared on Dan's left cheek.

Dan wrapped both arms around his head to protect his face. "By God, it's not right." His voice was muffled. "Not to give a man a decent chance."

Hale grew angrier by the second. "Like the one you gave me when you kicked me?" he shouted.

Hale was getting too mad, Cal thought. That hulk on his knees before Hale wasn't nearly as helpless as he was making himself sound. "Don't get yourself so worked up, Hale, that you forget to watch him," Cal warned.

Dan lowered his arms from his head and held out placating hands toward Hale. "Now just a minute," he started. He dived from his knees without trying to finish his words.

Cal was right in his estimation of Dan. "Hale," he yelled in warning. Dan intended to crash his body into Hale's legs, then smother him under his weight. If that happened, Cal would have to take an active hand.

The warning wasn't needed. Hale wasn't lulled for a moment. He stayed where he was, only lifting a knee to meet Dan's dive. Dan's face crashed against the raised knee, and Cal winced at the sound of crunching flesh. Maybe a broken bone or two was also in that sound.

Hale had lifted his knee at the exact moment of contact, timing his movement perfectly. The awesome force lifted Dan and knocked him over backwards. He landed on his back; his hands opened and closed, but those movements weren't directed.

Cal looked around. Bill hadn't moved. Meyers had run a little way, then stopped. He stood as though transfixed, his open mouth looking as though there were no supporting muscles in his face. He shuddered and with a visible effort managed to pull himself together. He cast one last frightened look on the two brothers, then whirled and ran, his short legs pumping as fast as he could make them go.

Hale took a step after him, and Cal's outflung arm stopped him. "Isn't your anger satisfied yet?"

Hale grinned sheepishly. "I guess it is. I couldn't catch him anyway." He used a thumb joint to dab at a trickle of blood from the corner of his mouth. He looked down at Dan and said almost apologetically. "That big bastard was tougher than I figured. He might have kicked me to pieces before I ever got back on my feet." While he said it as lightly as he could, his face was sober.

"Did he break any bones when he kicked you?" Cal asked. At the startled flash in Hale's eyes, he added, "I thought I saw you wince."

Hale felt his ribs. "I thought I felt something give," he admitted. He drew a deep breath and broke it off with a sudden gasp. There was a tight, white line around his lips. "Something down there just cussed me out good," he confessed.

Cal nodded. He was afraid of that. "We'll find somebody to give it a look," he said matter-of-factly. He looked at his right hand. Damned if it wasn't beginning to swell. He flexed it a few times and set his jaw at the stab of protest that ran through the hand. A hand bone could be so brittle. He grinned at Hale. "If we can find a doc, I want him to look at this hand, too."

Hale's face was apprehensive. "If Pardee gets up here and finds both of us laid up—" He didn't have to finish it. Cal's look showed he'd been thinking the same thought.

"What do you want to do with them?" Hale asked, jerking his head toward the two unconscious bodies.

"Do you feel charitable enough to want to do something for them?" Cal asked.

"Hell, no," Hale said with fervor.

"About the way I feel," Cal answered. His eyes danced with wicked glee. "Welcome to Evarts, Hale."

The despondency on Hale's face could be scraped off with a stick. He looked at the handful of nondescript buildings, and moral indignation was in his voice. "Do you call that a town?"

"I think it's going to be," Cal said seriously. "With all those herds coming up this railroad, it can't help but grow."

Chapter Three

CAL HAD EVARTS low rated with his first glimpse of it. It still wasn't much more than an annoying mote in a man's eyes, but he could see evidence of growth. A few of the buildings had that yellow look of new lumber.

He stopped a man approaching them and asked, "Could you tell us if there's a doctor in town?"

The short, dumpy man eyed Cal and Hale speculatively and said, "More cowboys."

Cal could sense Hale's bridling, but before he could open his mouth the man said, "It's a welcome relief to see a few white men instead of Indians." He added hastily, "That doesn't mean I've got anything against Indians or breeds—" He gestured helplessly. "But a man just gets hungry to talk to somebody who speaks his language."

Cal nodded his understanding. He guessed there was no place where a man could go without running into prejudice. Up here, it seemed to be against the Indians. Texans had a quick temper where Mexicans were concerned.

This was a garrulous man. Cal thought he would stand here the rest of the day, if he didn't prod him. "About that doctor," he said.

"We've got Doc Mathews. He's living in Evarts'

only hotel. Can't miss it," the man said. "Biggest, ugliest building in town." He pointed to a building at the end of the block. "Hits you right in the eye, don't it? Everybody told Hobart he was jumping the gun, but he couldn't wait to get that hotel built. He tried to tell everybody, with all that land leasing, this country had to grow." He reflectively rubbed his chin. "Maybe it takes that kind of belief to bring growth."

That land leasing talk was right down Cal's alley. "Much leasing going on?" he asked.

"Sure as hell is. Almost every day the Strip is full of beef. If the railroad can believe enough to build that strip, maybe Hobart had more vision than the rest of us. Every dollar he owns is in that hotel." His cackle had a tinge of malice. "There she sits. Twenty empty rooms. The only trouble is that the cow outfits just keep passing through." He sighed and shook his head. "Maybe they'll have to come back here and buy their supplies."

"Sure they will," Cal said.

Hale fidgeted impatiently beside Cal. All this talk was boring him. Hale was only interested in surface appearances. To him, Evarts was a dreary, little town. If there were pulsating throbs of growth beneath that surface, Hale would never dig far enough to discover them.

"Cal, my side hurts," he complained.

Cal smiled apologetically. "We'd better go find Mathews."

Alarm touched the man's face. "Hope it ain't too serious." At Cal's frown he said hastily, "Oh, the Doc's good enough. If you don't break into his drinking hours."

"What's his drinking hours?" Cal demanded.

"I guess you'd be on the safe side if you said any waking hour is a drinking hour."

Cal chuckled and thrust out a hand. "Thanks, Mister. I'm Cal Decker. This is my brother, Hale."

He felt the soft pressure of the plump hand. This hand hadn't known much manual labor.

"I'm Hy Simmons. I run a general store here." His face brightened with eagerness. "If you need anything, I've got it."

"We'll keep that in mind," Cal said gravely. He nodded to Simmons and moved on.

"Mouthy," Hale grunted.

Cal's eyebrows rose, but he let that pass. Simmons was a friendly little cuss, ready to offer help. Cal had never found that a bad trait in any man. Hale wouldn't find anything favorable in this country even if an angel suddenly stood before him. Hale had set his heart and head that there was no place like Texas, and nothing was going to change him. Cal had seen little of this country yet, but it looked good to him. At least, everything was green and lush. After looking at those sun baked, parched Texas acres for so long, anything that had life in it would look good to him.

"So you don't like the country, the town, or the people in it," Cal said drily. "But so far you can't say it's dull. He grinned at Hale's oath.

They walked into the hotel where a slender man sat behind the desk. Probably Hobart, Cal thought. From what Simmons said Cal doubted Hobart had enough money to hire even a clerk to staff an empty hotel. Hobart's face was too bright and eager and Cal knew what Hobart was thinking—here come a couple of cash customers.

Cal hated to wipe that eagerness off of Hobart's face, but it had to be done.

Hobart confirmed that first impression, for he stood and stuck out a hand. "I'm Sam Hobart. Happy to welcome you to Evarts' finest hotel."

Hale must have been hurting bad to cause him to speak caustically, but Cal knew that Hale wasn't always too careful about stepping on somebody's toes. Hale snorted and said sourly, "Owning the only hotel in town is the only reason that lets you claim that. Hell, I've seen a lot of barns I'd rather stay in."

The hard pound of running feet turned Cal's head. That kind of a rush was caused only by one of two things: anger or pure fright.

A young girl came flying out of a door behind Hobart. She might have topped five feet, but she wouldn't have had any margin left. There was enough anger packed into that small frame to fill a half-dozen larger women. She was red haired and freckle-faced, but looking at her Cal thought the freckles were for decoration. Somewhere under twenty, he thought and his eyes filled with admiration. Her eyes were so narrowed with anger Cal couldn't be sure of their color, but figured with that red hair she had to have green eyes. Her wrath was awesome, but it only amused Cal. Maybe it was because her anger was directed solely at Hale.

She stopped before Hale, her hands on her hips. By rising on her toes she was able to thrust her chin into Hale's face.

"I heard that," she stormed. "I'm damned sick of you cow people coming in here and criticizing everything you see. My father and I built this hotel, and we're damned proud of it."

"Here now, Ellie," Hobart said uneasily.

Father and daughter, Cal concluded. Hobart had obviously experienced her anger before, and he was a little awed by it.

"I'll handle this, Sam," she snapped.

Hale blinked several times under the ferocity of her attack. All during the long ride Hale had complained at having to leave Texas. Cal had heard him say over and over, "Just when I was getting someplace with Amity."

Even with her anger, this girl was something to see. She was small but beautifully made, and Cal could imagine how she would look when she smiled. He'd bet that all thoughts of Amity were swept from his brother's mind.

It was time to step in before Ellie flayed Hale some more, but before Cal could speak, Ellie contemptuously said, "We're filled up. Go find a barn to sleep in."

Cal heard Hobart's little distressed sound of protest. Business was poor, and here Ellie was turning down potential customers.

"I'm Cal Decker," he said. "My brother didn't mean what he said. He's been hurt. We weren't looking for rooms. We were told Dr. Mathews lives here. Is he in?"

Ellie chewed on her lower lip. Evidently, she was sorry to hear Hale was hurt, but she was still too angry to apologize.

She looked at Cal for the first time. He thought he passed her initial judgment favorably; at least, she didn't appear to be quite as angry.

"He does," Ellie said. "He doesn't have the good taste you two have." She whirled on her heels and retreated to the door, her shoulders squared.

"Who in the hell does she think she is?" Hale said furiously.

"Hold it, Hale," Cal warned. His brother had already offended these people or, at least, one of them. "Could we see the doctor?" he asked Hobart.

Hobart's face had crumpled into ruin, looking like a man whose burden had suddenly become too heavy. "He's in, though I don't know whether or not he'll see you," he said dully.

"We can find out, can't we?" Hale persisted angrily.

Hobart nodded slowly. He's in the first room to the right, at the head of the stairs."

"Thanks," Cal said softly. He looked back after they were halfway up the stairs. Hobart sat staring straight ahead. He's too beaten to show resentment, Cal thought and felt pity for the man. Hobart had the look of one who faced a blank wall with no way of getting through it.

"Pleased with yourself, Hale?" he asked acidly.

Cal expected the question to refire Hale's temper, but instead, Hale only looked miserable.

"She had no cause to jump me like that," Hale moaned. "Dammit, I didn't know she was anywhere around, or—"

"Or you wouldn't have said what you did," Cal said and grinned. Just those few seconds of confrontation with the girl had hit Hale hard. Cal could appreciate that. He'd looked at Ellie, too. If he could get into Hale's mind right now, he'd bet that Hale couldn't even remember what Amity looked like.

"How do you feel?" he asked.

He was asking about Hale's physical shape, not his emotional being, but Hale took it the other way.

"Like I been ridden hard and put away wet," he answered. He tried to meet Cal's eyes and couldn't. "I'm going to apologize to her the first chance I get."

"If she'll let you," Cal said drily, as he stopped before the first door on the right at the head of the stairs.

In answer to Cal's knock, a crusty voice called out, "It isn't locked."

Cal quirked his eyebrows. There wasn't any good humor in this hotel today.

Cal opened the door and stepped inside, Hale on his heels. It was a bare, little room, furnished with only the absolute necessities of living. A man, slouched in the only chair, finished pouring himself a drink and set the bottle on the floor beside the chair.

The doctor was old, at least in his mid sixties. His face was seamed, the flesh hanging loosely from it. He had white hair, and even the bushy eyebrows were colorless. He looked at Cal and Hale through rheumy and faded eyes as he finished his drink.

"Wrong time," he stated.

Cal grinned, remembering what Simmons had said. Maybe Dr. Mathews didn't usually mix his drinking hours with business, but he was doing so today. Simmons hadn't mentioned another doctor in town.

"Doc," Cal said firmly. "My brother's been hurt. He's got a side that needs looking after." He glanced at his own hand. It had swollen appreciably. "I've got a hand that needs some attention."

Those eyes weren't as faded as Cal had first thought, for they were sharp in their appraisal.

Mathews sighed and stood. "Damned nuisance," he complained. He motioned at the chair he had just vacated. "Sit down here."

His manner rankled Hale, and he snapped, "Don't put yourself out for me."

Cal pushed Hale down into the chair. "Shut up," he commanded. "He's not in the best of moods this morning, Doc. He's got a bum side."

"Take off your shirt," Mathews ordered. As Hale made no move to obey, Mathews shrugged and said, "Hell, it suits me just fine."

Cal had about all he could stand of Hale's irascibility. "You heard him," he said sharply.

Hale locked eyes with Cal, then slowly began unbuttoning his shirt.

"He always this pleasant?" Mathews asked sourly.

"Like you are," Cal said evenly. He expected Mathews to flare, but instead Mathews' lips twitched and he chuckled.

"Tough ain't you?" he asked.

"Tough enough," Cal said calmly.

"We'll get along," Mathews replied. His hands moved along Hale's side, the fingers pressing and probing.

Hale winced, and a white line appeared around his mouth. "Just a minute. I'll lie down on the floor and you can jump up and down on me."

"Might not be a bad idea," Mathews growled. He looked at Cal. "How'd he get this?"

"Kicked." As Mathews eyebrows formed question marks, Cal explained, "A couple of railroad hands decided we needed mannering."

"From what I've heard looks like they had the right idea," Mathews said tartly. He probed and pushed a little more, then ordered, "Take a deep breath. Another. That hurt?"

"Hell yes, it hurts," Hale said hotly.

"What's wrong, Doc?" Cal asked as Mathews straightened.

"Broken ribs," Mathews said tersely. "At least two of them. I could feel the ends grinding together."

"Oh, goddammit," Cal exploded. "We've got work to do."

"He won't be much help with those," Mathews said flatly.

"Can he ride?"

Mathews shook his head. "He can, but he shouldn't. I can bind them up, and it'll help him some. But the best thing he can do is to rest and give those ribs time to heal."

"How long?" Cal demanded.

Mathews opened his bag and pulled out a roll of bandage. "Depends on how fast he heals." He began wrapping the bandage around Hale's body. After a couple of times around he asked, "Too tight?"

"Would that bother you?" Hale snarled.

"Must be a joy to be around him all the time," Mathews said acidly. His deft fingers never slackened their work.

Cal nodded. He wouldn't have blamed Mathews if he backhanded Hale across the mouth. "But he's not always this bad, Doc. He hurts, and he's just been throwed by a red-headed filly."

Mathews stopped long enough to look up at Cal, and his eyes twinkled. "Ah," he said knowingly. "He ran into Ellie."

Cal saw the cuss words forming on Hale's lips,

and he snapped, "Hold it. You earned her tongue lashing." He looked at Mathews. "He ran down Hobart's hotel, and Ellie overheard him."

Mathews cackled in appreciation. "She's got a tongue like a cactus pad, hasn't she?" His face sobered. "Don't blame her. She's scared. Sam put every dime he had into building this hotel when he heard about the leasing of the reservations. He figured it would open up the country. That would mean a lot of people would need someplace to stay. The railroad believes the same way. The big difference is they've got money behind them. Sam doesn't. His trouble is that he built about six months too early. He rushed in to be first. If they hang on, they'll make it."

Mathews finished his bandaging and stepped back. "Take a deep breath now."

Hale did as he was told, and Mathews asked, "That any better?"

"A lot." Hale breathed deeply again. "That took the knife out of my guts. Doc, I want to apologize for—"

Mathews slapped him on the shoulder, cutting off Hale's words. "Wasting your time. Wouldn't recognize an apology if I heard one. You do just as I tell you. Give those ribs plenty of rest." He turned toward Cal. "You said something about a hand that needs looking at."

Cal extended the hand, his face glum.

"Does my diagnosis of your brother make you that unhappy?" Mathews asked.

"Hell no," Cal protested. "I'm grateful it's no worse but we do have a lot of work ahead. My father leased some of that Indian reservation land. When he heard the Bureau of Indian Affairs was opening it up, he moved fast. He sent in his bid to Washington, and with a senator's influence, got hold of a piece of it. Pardee sent us up here early to look it over. When a drought clamps down, you either make a move or lose your cattle, so Pardee's shipping our cattle up here. When we left Texas, he thought he'd be up here a week or ten days after us. He'll be plumb upset when he finds out we haven't done what he ordered us to do."

Hale stood and rocked his shoulders. "See! I can move as well as I ever did."

Mathews flung Hale an annoyed glance. "You don't listen very well, do you? You want one of those rib ends poking through you? If it does, you'll be laid up a hell of a lot longer than I told you."

His fingers poked at Cal's hand. The pressure sent a stab of pain up Cal's arm, but he kept his face stolid.

Mathews pressed harder. "You trying to prove something? Stop acting brave on me. Tell me when it hurts."

"It hurts," Cal admitted.

"Good," Mathews said briskly.

Why, you old bastard, Cal thought. You can say that. It's me hurting. Not you.

Mathews finished his examination, and his face was grave. "Hate to give you the bad news."

Oh God, Cal thought in dismay. He's found a broken bone. Pardee is going to raise pure hell when he hears how Hale and I got busted up. "Go ahead," he grunted.

Mathews grinned with fiendish delight. "I can't find any broken bones."

"Why, you miserable old—" Cal broke off his words and couldn't help grinning.

Mathews cackled again. "I got to get some pleasure out of this business, don't I?" His eyes twinkled. "The hand's swollen and it'll be sensitive for a couple of days. Use some common sense, and it'll be all right."

Mathews sat down in his chair. "I'd offer you two a drink, but I've got only one glass."

"That never stopped either of us," Cal said promptly.

He took the proffered bottle, and Mathews said, "Sit on the bed."

Cal handed Hale the bottle, and Hale swigged down a generous drink. Something in Mathews' covert interest should have warned Hale to use a little caution, but the word wasn't in Hale's vocabulary.

Hale choked and gasped, and his eyes watered. "My God," he said feebly after he got his breath back. "That's the worst stuff I ever tasted."

"Ain't it?" Mathews agreed with smug pleasure. "It takes a man to handle whiskey with that much wallop."

Cal was forewarned, and he took a smaller drink. He rolled it around in his mouth, trying to adjust his palate to the onslaught of the whiskey. Even that didn't fully prepare him. Mathews understated it when he said this whiskey carried a wallop. It burned all the way down, and it kicked around in Cal's stomach like a berserk mule. Cal might have been able to keep his face straight, but he couldn't keep the tears from welling into his eyes.

"That stuff could make a man swear off of drinking whiskey," Cal said as he handed the bottle back to Mathews.

Mathews took the bottle back and half filled his

glass. "Never stopped me." In proof he emptied the glass without hesitation.

"The one reason I came up here," he said mournfully, "was to get away from a lot of bothersome patients. All you cattlemen will change all that I guess. You two couldn't even step off a train without getting banged around. I guess they'll be coming after me day and night to patch up some idiot that got himself broken up."

Hale was getting mad again, and Cal stepped in. "Doc, I hope you don't pick up and go," Cal said softly.

"By God, that's what I just might do," Mathews said fiercely.

Cal grinned at him. The old man's toughness was only a thin veneer. Cal had seen how quickly it was stripped off when Mathews found out they were hurt.

"If business doesn't make you happy, Doc, you should be glad for Hobart and Ellie," Cal said. "All these people coming in are bound to help them."

"I guess I can stand it, if it does Ellie and Sam some good," Mathews grumbled. "But for a man to lose his privacy is a hell of a price to pay."

Cal watched Mathews with awe. He didn't know how many drinks Mathews had before he and Hale came into the room, but to his personal knowledge he had seen Mathews drink enough to put an ordinary man flat on his back. Mathews must have the capacity of a water tank.

Mathews down his drink and asked, "How many cattle is your old man bringing in?"

"Around eight thousand head," Cal answered absently. "I don't see how the railroad can do it.

They offered Pardee free transportation for those cattle."

"You're one of the small outfits," Mathews jeered.

"Big enough," Cal answered, ruffled. That number of cattle had been big in their part of Texas where three hungry mouths eating every blade of grass had seemed too much. "It's going to take a lot of cars to carry that cattle. That's going to cost the railroad."

"Don't think those railroad officials deserve saint robes," Mathews said drily. "They know what they're doing. I never heard of a railroad ever giving away a damned thing. Those boys sat down and saw three million acres of empty land and figured out how they could get some dollars out of those acres. They didn't have to look too far to come up with an answer. Fill up those empty acres with cattle. Those cattle will have to be shipped back to markets when they're ready, won't they?" Mathews grinned wolfishly at Cal's nod. "That's when you'll find out how saintly they are. You'll be stuck plenty."

"Maybe," Cal replied. He wasn't going to quarrel with the railroad over shipping charges. Without the railroad, Cal knew where the Deckers would be. At the moment, the Deckers were alive and it was all due to the railroad.

"From what I've heard, we're not the only damned idiots," Cal said lightly. "Lots of outfits already in ahead of us."

Mathews nodded. "The railroad has kept their part of the bargain so far," he said grudgingly. "I'll admit they've spent a pile of money to entice you cattlemen here. Have you seen the Strip yet?"

Hale was beginning to fidget again. Cal frowned at him. He didn't give a damn how itchy Hale was getting; he wanted to hear all he could about this new land. "I've heard about it, but I haven't seen it. I haven't even unloaded the horses yet."

Mathews nodded in understanding. "Your eyes'll pop out when you see the Strip. If the Milwaukee Railroad was going to run a spur to Evarts, they did everything they could to make Evarts attractive as a shipping point. They had a lease on the whole north tier of townships. They fenced in a six-mile wide lane on both sides. That lane is eighty miles long. When a trail boss hits the Strip, he knows he has it made."

Cal whistled softly. "The railroad thought of everything."

"Just about," Mathews said gloomily. "Except how to keep the people from coming here." He reached for the bottle again. "Sure you won't have another drink."

Hale shuddered, and Cal said, "I'll pass this time. How much do we owe you, Doc?"

"Oh hell," Mathews said wearily as though the whole subject of finances wearied him. "I didn't do much. How does a dollar sound to you?"

Cal reached into his pocket and pulled out a bill. "Cheap, Doc." He started to leave the room and paused. "Doc, is there somebody around who knows this country? I've got to look over the land we leased and I don't even know where it is."

"Look up Joe Longbraids," Mathews said promptly. "He knows this country like the back of his hand. He should. He was born and raised here."

Mathews bristled at Cal's look of doubt. "That

name get to you? You only have to dislike three quarters of him. He's three-quarters Sioux."

"It's not that at all," Cal denied quickly. "I was just wondering if he would know where the Decker lease is."

"He will," Mathews assured him. "He knows everything that's going on in this country."

"Then he's my man," Cal said. "Where will I find him?"

"He works odd hours at the blacksmith shop. If he's not there, Hawkins will know where he can be found."

Cal leaned over and extended his hand. "I'm not saying any thanks. It's been a pleasure to know you."

Mathews grinned sardonically. "I wonder what the railroad men found wrong with your manners. Drop by any time when it's purely social."

"I hope to God I can keep it that way," Cal said soberly.

Mathews pointed a finger at Hale. "You remember what I told you about knocking those ribs around. You and I didn't get along too well. Damned if I want to go through that again."

Hale grinned. "I'll keep that in mind."

Hale waited until he and Cal were going down the hall before he spoke. "Rough old rooster, isn't he?"

Before Cal could bristle at the implied criticism, Hale went on, "But he grows on you. Like a damned wart. It's a nuisance and you know it's there, but you can get used to it."

Cal grinned. Hale had summed up the Doc pretty well. "I'm leaving in the morning. What are you going to do?"

Hale made a production of his thinking. "I've got to follow the doc's orders, don't I? Do you think Ellie would rent me a room until you get back?"

"Ah," Cal said knowingly. So Ellie had made a dent in Hale's cocky exterior. He was trying to cover his real feelings and was doing a poor job of it.

"Let's go see," Hale replied. Cal felt a vague sense of loss. Damn Hale. The older he grew the more he became a rival in everything.

"You watch your mouth," Cal advised. "Or you'll be sleeping under the skies."

"You don't have to be on my back all the time," Hale said heatedly.

Chapter Four

ELLIE WAS BEHIND the desk when Cal approached it the next morning. Hobart had rented them a room and had shown no resentment, only a pathetic eagerness.

Overwhelmed with admiration, Cal slowed his approach. Ellie was prettier than a new born filly. Her head was down, absorbed in some work, and she hadn't seen him yet. Cal wondered how she had accepted the fact that he and Hale were guests in her hotel.

"Morning," he said, and his smile softened the craggier aspects of his face.

Ellie looked up and for a moment, her face stiffened. "Good morning," she returned. "Was your night bearable?"

Cal winced, but managed to hold onto his smile. Underneath that eye-pleasing exterior was a solid layer of flint.

"We had a good night," he said heartily. "My brother's still asleep."

Ellie didn't sniff, but Cal felt she wanted to.

What's it going to take to melt her, he wondered. Maybe an outright apology would do it.

He drew a deep breath and plunged in earnestly. "I sure regret what Hale said yesterday, but he was hurting and—"

"Short tempered," she finished tartly.

"Yes," Cal said evenly. "We found out he had some broken ribs. Doc Matthews fixed him up."

For the first time Ellie looked fully at him. He had been right about those eyes being green. At this moment, they were distressed. She did have feeling. That layer of flint was thinning.

"I'm so sorry," she said. "I didn't know. He's going to be all right?"

"Sure," Cal replied. "Doc said he has to take it easy for a week or so. He doesn't want Hale doing much moving around. He'll stay here unless—" And he smiled. "Unless you throw him out."

She tried to keep from smiling and couldn't. She had a beautiful smile. Laughter was welling up behind her eyes, making them sparkle.

The smile did it. It kicked Cal full in the stomach, leaving him feeling breathless and hollow.

"Did you think I would?" she asked.

"I didn't know," Cal answered gravely.

"No, both of you are welcome here." That grim little undernote was in her voice again. This time it said that Ellie and Hobart weren't doing well enough to be picky.

"I know Hale wants to apologize to you," "Don't be too rough on him."

"I won't," she promised and laughed again. She glanced at the registration book lying before her. "Mr. Decker," she finished.

That promise brought gloom to Cal. Hale would have all that time here while Cal was gone. Hale had a lot of charm when he wanted to use it. That scared the hell out of Cal.

"I've got to be gone for a while," he said. "Pa

THE RAGGED EDGE 41

leased some of that Indian reservation land. I haven't even seen it yet."

If she was interested, she fooled him. "I hope you find just what you want, Mr. Decker."

Cal echoed that wish fevently. The only trouble was they were thinking of different things. He started to move on and checked himself. "Doc Mathews told me to look up Joe Longbraids. Know where I can find him?"

He was turning into a fraud, he thought wryly. Mathews had already given him that information. Cal was just grabbing at anything to prolong this conversation.

"He's in town," she replied. "I saw him earlier this morning."

"Thank you." Cal swore at himself because he sounded as though she had just handed him half the world.

"Would he guide me? Doc says he knows this country well."

She had a cute habit of wrinkling her forehead when she weighed a problem. "I know he's guided other people. I don't see why he'd turn you down."

"Have you heard what he's been paid?"

Again her forehead wrinkled. "I think he gets two dollars a day, plus his feed."

Cal nodded solemn agreement. "Can't squawk about that." He still sought for a reason to stay longer and knew he was making a damned fool of himself. "Well," he said lamely. "I'd better go and see if I can find him. I'll see you when I return."

She nodded without speaking her attention already back to her paper work.

Cal looked back from the doorway. She wasn't

watching him at all. You poor damn fool, he told himself.

His anger mounted as he walked down the street, mostly at himself, but he had enough left over to spill onto Hale. Damn you, Hale. You would have to be the one who got your ribs broken.

He didn't have any trouble finding the blacksmith shop. It was a ramshackle shed at the outskirts of town. Cal grinned in sour amusement. That wouldn't put it very far away from the very heart of Evarts.

A man was pounding vigorously at the anvil as Cal entered. He was about as good a physical specimen as Cal had ever ever seen. His shoulders were broad, tapering to a small, hard waist, and with each swing of the hammer, the bicep muscles rippled. The man wore his hair in Indian fashion, the long braids reaching to his chest. Cal knew he had found his man.

The rhythm of the hammering never broke. Longbraids didn't look at Cal, but he knew Cal was here, because those black eyes had flicked over him once.

Cal waited patiently until Longbraids laid down the hammer.

"Some work you want done?" Longbraids asked.

He spoke English well, and that was a relief. Cal would have no trouble communicating with him. The high cheekbones, the hawk nose and black eyes yelled Indian. Whatever white blood was in Longbraids was well hidden.

"I'm Cal Decker," Cal said, extending his hand. "You're Joe Longbraids, aren't you?"

Longbraids nodded without reaching for Cal's hand. That irritated Cal until he remembered what somebody once told him: Indians didn't like to be touched, particularly by a white man.

Cal dropped his hand. All right, he shrugged, if that's the way he wants it. Those black eyes weighed Cal carefully, and Cal had the impression of a wild animal's wariness in them. Longbraids would be hard to get to know.

"You the D bar S brand?" Longbraids asked.

Cal nodded. The Doc was right, Longbraids was up on what was happening. The D was for Decker, the S for Sarah, Cal's mother.

That watchful waiting grated on Cal. Longbraids spoke good English, but he sure didn't use much of it. "The cattle are coming in next week," Cal said. "I haven't seen the land my father leased. Do you know where it is?"

Longbraids nodded.

Cal's irritation was mounting. He had to dig for every word he got out of Longbraids. "Will you take me over it?"

That could have been a flicker of amusement in Longbraids' eyes at the white man's impatience. "Yes. I have to finish this job. I'll be ready to go in an hour."

"Will two dollars a day be all right?" Cal asked, trying to keep his voice even.

Longbraids nodded again. He picked up his hammer and said, "I'll meet you at the stockyards."

"Good," Cal muttered, unable to keep the bite out of his voice. If this Indian didn't want to be friendly, it was all right with him.

"I'll be waiting for you," he said. He walked out

without waiting for Longbraids' answer. He didn't expect one.

The stockyards . . . Evarts' one distinctive feature. It was built on the eastern bank of the Missouri River, and although Cal had been there last night, it was too near dark for him to fully appreciate the magnitude of the yards. Cattle pens lined the river bank for a long way in both directions and Cal couldn't begin to guess how many cattle these pens could hold. Each pen had its own chute, and train rails ran along side of them. The railroad was obviously preparing to go into the cattle handling business in a big way.

Cal stared across the river. He still wasn't in South Dakota. Evarts was in Minnesota. Cal would have to cross that wide expanse of water before he could say he'd reached his new home.

He looked appraisingly at the ferry boat landing. The boat wasn't in sight. Good God! Was that the only way to get a heard of cattle across that muddy, roily stream? It must be, because Mathews said several other outfits had already arrived.

Cal became absorbed watching a huge log churning down the river. Some great force worked on it, constantly turning it over and over, now and then whirling it around end to end. Occasionally the current pulled the log completely under, then it would surface again a good twenty or thirty yards down stream. Cal shuddered at the force of a current that could handle the huge log as though it was no more than a match stick.

Cal hadn't realized any one was near him until the man spoke. "Don't know how many hours I've spent watching this old bitch. She changes every ten seconds. She ain't pretty, but she sure can fascinate you."

"Yes," Cal acknowledged. He looked at Lem Fellows. Fellows, the manager of the yards, was a thin, bandy-legged man with a bad limp. He didn't speak of the accident that caused the limp, and Cal didn't ask about it. Probably a range accident, Cal had thought last night when he had made arrangements for the horses to be unloaded and taken care of. Fellows' knowledge of horses and cattle had to have been gained through practical experience.

"I know what you mean," Cal answered. "Is a ferryboat the only means of getting across the river?"

Fellows grinned cheerfully. One side of his face was misshapen because of the huge cud of tobacco always tucked in his cheek. He spat an amber stream and laughed. "Felt the same scare when I first looked at her. You wouldn't believe how many cattle have already crossed that way." His face was solemn, but his eyes danced. "Don't worry. If the boat goes under while you're aboard, it'll be a first."

"That's a help," Cal said sardonically.

Fellows slapped his leg. "Thought you'd think so," he chortled. "Your horses're doing just fine. But one of them is a real bastard. He kicked the shit out of one of my men this morning."

Cal frowned at him. "That's Troublemaker. I told you to keep an eye on him."

"I know," Fellows grunted, then grinned. "But you didn't say a real big eye. Puff'll be limping around for a few days. He was just lucky he wasn't standing a couple of inches closer, or that leg would've been shattered."

"I'm glad to hear it's no worse," Cal said and meant it. He didn't want little things going wrong from the start. He wouldn't call himself a superstitious man, but small mishaps were like leaves flying in a wind, portending the arrival of a storm. Maybe it's already started, he thought soberly. Naw, he disclaimed. That little set-to with the railroad men was just a difference of opinion. It couldn't be counted.

"I hired Longbraids to take me over our lease," Cal said, and then waited to see if Fellows would let the remark die there or expound on it at great length.

"Couldn't have hired a better man," Fellows said promptly.

"Sure doesn't talk much," Cal remarked. He couldn't keep the caustic note out of his voice.

"So you've found that out already. Lot of lessons have taught him that you don't trust first and get your experience afterwards."

"He's got a damned suspicious, standoff way," Cal grumbled.

"Comes from a long line of suspicious people," Fellows said gravely. "His father was killed in that Custer mess."

"But I had no part in that," Cal protested. "Hell, I wasn't even born."

"He knows that," Fellows said quietly. "But our kind of people did take part. Sure, all that's done for good. But it's built up that watchfulness you're complaining about. The Sioux learned a real hard lesson. They've got to be convinced that respect is there before they can trust."

"I see," Cal said softly. Maybe he had some learning to do, too. "He's to meet me here in a hour."

"Then he'll be here," Fellows replied. "You taking the horses out today?"

"Two of them. I need a saddle and a pack horse. I might as well give Troublemaker a workout. If I miss a few days, he gets meaner than hell."

Fellow shook his head. "I don't envy you. He's got that look in his eyes."

Cal grinned. That wasn't news to him. "He's a lot of horse when he gets that first cussedness knocked out of him. I might as well get it over before Longbraids gets here."

Troublemaker didn't cause any trouble while he was being saddled. He stood there almost droopy, unless you happened to look at his eyes. They were rolling, and too much muddy white showed. The ever-growing wicked glaze was the final summary. Here was a handful of hell, just waiting to get back at his tormentor.

"Twist his ear," Cal said to Fellows before he reached for the horn.

Troublemaker squalled at the pain of his twisted ear, and Cal swung up, pulled his hat down over his ears and called, "Let him go."

Hell broke loose all around Cal as Troublemaker hunkered down, his muscles rigid as slabs of iron. Cal had ridden this wild one so many times that he knew its tricks, but he never dared to relax. Everytime he had, Cal had busted the ground with his butt. He was filled with so much tension that it was difficult to breath. He raked Troublemaker with a long swipe of the spurs and said, "Let's go."

Troublemaker exploded like a case of dynamite going off all at once. He never tried to cover much ground with his bucking. He stayed in one spot, trying to drive each hoof print deeper into the ground. Cal grunted with each slam of the saddle against his butt. Vaguely, he heard excited yelling. Troublemaker must be putting on his usual good show.

Troublemaker had a cute trick of landing on one stiffened foreleg, whipping his rear end around as he made contact. Cal got a savage jolt, and at the same time, his body was twisted in the opposite direction. His mouth opened wide as he gasped for breath. After three or four times of landing on one foreleg, Troublemaker began to vary his tactics by landing on both stiffened forelegs and kicking out with his rear heels as he made contact with the ground. The motion caught Cal going forward, as though he had run full speed into a stone wall. Then the kicking would whip his body backwards.

You miserable bastard, Cal thought mournfully. One would think after so much experience like this, Troublemaker would quit sooner. But each time, the ride was longer, or seemed so to Cal.

Troublemaker stopped all at once, his muscles loose, his head down and blowing. Cal waited for his world to settle down before he stiffly dismounted. He felt a familiar trickle of moisture at a nostril, and with a thumb joint wiped away the thin flow of blood. That too had happened before.

Cal slapped the horse affectionately on a shoulder. "You ol' devil," he said without resentment. Troublemaker did what he had to do, and to Cal that was a form of honesty.

Fellows came up to Cal, his eyes glowing. "Never saw a better ride. How often does this go on?"

"Only when I want to use him," Cal said plaintively. "Guess he'll never change."

"How many in your outfit ride him?" Fellows asked.

"He belongs to me," Cal said simply. He finished almost apologetically, "You see, I wind up with all the rough ones."

Fellows whistled softly. "You mean the other horses in the pen are in the same class?"

"Maybe not quite," Cal admitted. He let a hand rest on Troublemaker's withers. "This'll be some horse, if I can ever tame him down."

Fellows shook his head in unfeigned admiration. "Mister, I wouldn't trade jobs with you." He lowered his voice. "Longbraids is over there. He came up just as you climbed into the saddle."

Cal wondered what Longbraids thought about the ride. Did the ride earn him any respect in the Indian's eyes? He shook his head. It didn't matter; he wasn't here to try and build up a standing with Longbraids.

Longbraids swung down and came toward Cal. Cal couldn't see any change in that stoic expression, but he imagined the eyes showed a little warmth.

"Tough horse," Longbraids said tersely. "What's his name?"

"Troublemaker,"

Cal could almost swear Longbraids was going to grin. Instead, Longbraids said shortly. "Good name. Ready to go?"

"Ready," Cal replied. He was prepared for a long and silent ride.

Chapter Five

CAL SYMPATHIZED WITH Troublemaker and the pack horse. He wasn't very crazy about going on that ferry, either. Longbraid's horse didn't show the slightest concern. Evidently, he had made enough trips on the boat to have become used to it.

The ferry was a floating stockyard, built in a series of pens. Cal judged each of those pens could hold up to forty head of cattle. The pens kept the cattle separated and prevented them from bunching up in one spot, putting too much weight on any one side of the boat. It was going to be a slow, tedious job moving a big bunch of cattle across the river.

Troublemaker lost his fear and began nibbling at a flake of hay. Cal decided he could safely leave him, and he walked over to the rail where Longbraids stood.

"More water than I've ever seen at one time," Cal said. "Wish we'd had some of this spread out over where I came from."

Longbraids continued staring at the water. Cal could feel his face heating up at the continued silence. To hell with him, he thought.

"A big river," Longbraids finally said. And, again, there was that long pause.

My God, Cal thought. It sure takes him a long time to find a few words to say.

"A hard river," Longbraids continued. "Nobody can afford to be careless around it. This old river has a long list of men and animals to answer for."

Was this a subtle warning? Cal didn't know. But at least, Longbraids was talking.

"It must take forever to move a herd over this river," said Cal.

Longbraids shook his head, the movement barely perceptible, "Quicker than you'd think. The Cross T moved ten thousand head across this river not over two weeks ago."

That gave Cal a sense of relief. If the Cross T could move that many, the D bar S shouldn't have any trouble with a lesser number of cattle.

Cal wanted to keep the conversation going. "My father leased twenty thousand acres of land out here." He wondered if that sounded like bragging because he hadn't intended it that way.

"I know," Longbraids said softly.

That made Cal feel like a fool, for while Longbraids didn't smile, Cal was sure he was secretly amused. Cal wanted to say he wasn't patronizing Longbraids, but decided, if he said more, it would only make matters worse.

"Don't worry. You haven't taken all of the land."

Cal frowned. Now he was sure his words had amused Longbraids.

"Over three million acres of land in Standing Rock and Cheyenne River Reservations."

This was the second time Cal had heard the figure. He was more impressed than ever, for instinctively, he sensed the breadth of Longbraids' knowledge.

"Do you know where D bar S land is?"

Longbraids nodded. His eyes switched back to the river and again he paused. Damnit, Cal thought heatedly. Do I have to pull every scrap of information out of him?

"D bar S land is on the southern side of the Strip in Cheyenne River Reservation," Longbraids said. "A day's ride down the Strip will take us to your gate."

Suddenly Cal forgave him for those long pauses. It was Longbraids' way, and Cal had no right to demand it be changed.

"Three million acres of grass," Cal repeated. The magnitude of such a vast reach of land filled him with awe. "My God, that's a cattleman's dream. They'll make a big change in this country."

"They did the first time," Longbraids said softly.

Cal didn't get that at all. This was the first time the reservation had been opened to cattlemen. What did Longbraids mean by the first time?

Longbraids studied Cal for a moment and appeared to be reading his mind. He said, "They weren't cattlemen the first time, but they were white men."

Cal felt the blood flow into his face. He got what Longbraids meant. "Yes," he said uncomfortably. He wanted to point out this arrangement was bound to help the Indians, because they would participate in the lease money flowing over the land. But maybe it was best he held his tongue. Longbraids knew about that. Once, the Indians had owned all this land. Leasing the reservation land was like a robber, who having stripped a wealthy man of everything he owned, was now tossing him a few pennies to show what a generous soul he was.

Longbraids must have sensed Cal's mental torment and changed the subject. "You have ridden Troublemaker before?"

The timbre of his voice hadn't changed, but Cal sensed that Longbraids wasn't holding him solely responsible for past abuses. He grinned and said, "A lot of times."

"You go through that each time?"

Cal nodded. "He's one stubborn horse."

"You must be one stubborn man," Longbraids said thoughtfully.

That was the first iota of respect Cal had detected in Longbraids' voice. Maybe things between them weren't going to be as bleak as he thought.

Cal smiled as he said, "Unlucky, I'd say. I've had a knack for sticking on a horse since I was knee-high to a grasshopper. Pa just started handing me the mean ones. Now, I wind up with all of them."

Again, Cal was aware of that quick, almost furtive appraisal. He wished he knew how Longbraids totalled up his findings.

"I'd like to try him some day," Longbraids said. His voice was a little strained as though asking embarrassed him.

"Why not?" Cal said promptly. "How about tomorrow morning?" Did that quick flicker in Longbraids' eyes say that startled him? Maybe, but Cal meant every word of it.

The remainder of the crossing was completed with hardly a word between them, but this time it didn't bother Cal. Some kind of contact had been established. If he didn't push too hard against this frail meeting of minds, it could grow. That was the white man's one big failing in dealing with others; he pushed too hard and too aggressively.

Cal led Troublemaker and the pack horse off of the ferry after it landed. He thought he saw surprise in Longbraids' eyes and explained, "Never know when he'll try it again. He's dumped me before. I don't want him throwing me into that river."

This time, Cal was sure a fleeting smile touched Longbraids' lips.

After they were on land, Cal mounted with no difficulty. Maybe the first lesson of the morning was still strong in the horse's head.

"We are in the Strip," Longbraids announced.

Cal looked about him. This didn't look any different from any other land. Then he remembered the Strip was supposed to be six miles wide. If he was anywhere near the middle of it, he couldn't expect to see the fences on either side.

Cal's heart swelled with elation, even in the Strip the grass was knee-high to Troublemaker. Those poor, half-starved D bar S beasts would go wild when they saw this. Once they were turned out on grass this good, they would be easy to handle. They would be too busy eating to have anything else in their heads.

"Good grass," he said as they started down the Strip.

"Eighty miles long," Longbraids said. "More than an ordinary ranch ever hopes to have. Your land adjoins the Strip. You can graze it several months out of the year, as long as other herds aren't using it to drive to market."

Cal felt like yelling his delight at the news. He didn't let his expression change. He didn't want Longbraids thinking, here was another crazy white man, but all this free grass was a pure windfall. He thought of the cattle that had gone down in Texas out of pure weakness from lack of food and were unable to get up. Surely that couldn't happen here. Cal felt as though he had suddenly been set down in paradise, and he cautioned himself against becoming complacent. If there wasn't the problem of ample feed, there would be other problems. He had never known a time when a cattleman wasn't besieged by trouble in one form or another.

"How far do we go before we turn in?" Cal asked. He had almost said "our land" and held the words in time. Longbraids might not show offense, but the phrase was bound to have an abrasive effect.

Twenty miles to the D bar S gate," Longbraids returned calmly.

Cal nodded without comment. Maybe Longbraids didn't wear his feelings on his sleeve, the way Cal feared.

They approached a fair sized lake and stopped to let the horses drink.

"Twelve miles from where we started," Longbraids said. "Water about every twelve miles along the Strip. Either lakes, creeks, or man-made watering holes. The railroad even put in several big dams to be sure there's water where it's needed."

The railroad had shown foresight. Twelve miles was just about a day's drive for a beef herd. While a herd was in the Strip, water problems simply couldn't exist. Cal thought wryly, he had started out cussing the railroad, and now here he was praising them.

Longbraids had been cutting a definite angle for the last half mile, and at Cal's glance said, "Riding over to the fence. D bar S land is on this side."

Cal nodded when he finally saw the fence. Again, he was filled with praise for the railroad. The fence was a four strand affair. Once a man turned his cattle behind that fence, he would no longer have to worry about them straying.

His expression brightened as he saw the wide gate in the fence ahead of him. Longbraids shook his head.

"Lazy V land," he grunted. "Next gate is your land."

Cal had to curb his impatience until they reached the second gate. He wanted to see D bar S land. He was like a kid on Christmas eve, unable to wait for Christmas morning.

Longbraids got down and opened the second gate. Cal knew his face was beaming with pleasure. Every step from now on would be taken on D bar S land. Pardee would go quietly, crazy with joy because he would never gaze on better grass. Hale might not show the same reaction, but Hale hadn't grown up yet.

Cal rode along, drinking in the beauties of his land. Most of it was a solid sea of wheat grass, belly-high to a horse. Good stands of timber interspersed the grass, and that delighted Cal even more. Those stands meant good wintering for the cattle. He identified some of the trees as they rode through the first stand. There was cottonwood, ash, and elm, and those thick copses were wild plum. The plum trees were a mass of blossoms, and their fragrance filled Cal's head. He had to ask Longbraids what the chokecherry and Juneberry thickets along the streams were. The wild roses were just bursting into full bloom and added their color and fragrance.

He kept nodding in delight as more of this land unfolded. So far, he had found nothing to fault it. It was well watered. They rarely rode more than a mile or two when another stream had to be crossed. Cal filed the location of each one in his head, remembering the fordable places Longbraids pointed out. Those streams presented no problem to a horseman, but in some places, they could be difficult for roundup wagons to cross.

Longbraids pointed out two of the largest buttes and named them, Twin and Dog. Cal wondered about the tall rock towers on top and asked about them. They didn't look like the work of nature.

"Indians built them," Longbraids answered, making no attempt to hide the quiet pride in his voice. "They mark permanent springs in the base of the buttes."

"Smart," Cal said and meant it. This was only another indication of how well the Indian knew this country. Those towers could be seen from a long way off. Right now, it didn't look as though this country ever suffered from lack of water, but Cal knew there would be dry spells here. Every country suffered such periods from time to time, and to a thirsty man, those towers were welcome beacons.

Cal couldn't keep the surprise from his face at the first sight of a house. It sat not fifty yards from a meandering creek, shadowed by tall cottonwoods. It was a massive structure, built of large cottonwood logs, the cracks between them daubed full of gumbo mud, which had dried to a soft gray color that blended well with the surroundings. The roof was covered with a thick layer of dirt. Cal was familiar with such buildings. They promised coolness in the summer and warmth in winter.

"Looks like it's empty," he commented.

Longbraids shrugged. "Has been the last two years. Old John Elk died then, and his wife couldn't live out here all by herself. After she left nobody moved in. Does a house in this land surprise you?" he asked sardonically. "Three thousand families are scattered over the reservations, and many of them have built such houses." The sardonic gleam in his eyes grew. "The Indian likes to keep warm and cool, too."

Cal chuckled, feeling no offense. Longbraids had a subtle way of driving a lesson home. Cal also marked the location of the house in his mind. If it was abandoned, he saw no reason why they couldn't use it as the ranch headquarters. A few pole corrals and maybe a barn or two would make this place entirely adequate. It would save the hard, long hours of building a new house and would immediately allow the D bar S to turn to the more important work of getting the herd established. This house could be a godsend.

"Do you suppose we could move into it?"

"Nobody to stop you," Longbraids answered. That sardonic note was still in his voice.

Cal looked back at the house as they rode away. Hale might snort at it in disdain, but then, Hale sometimes had delusions of grandeur.

"You will find cattle already here," Longbraids said. "Some of the Indian families run big herds, big enough for them to have their own roundups. The Indian Department says that the Indian is allowed a hundred head to graze free on each lease."

Cal was familiar with that clause in the lease. The leasees paid three cents an acre annually for his grass, but all cattle of the native inhabitants could not be disturbed. Longbraids had something else on his mind. Cal waited patiently. Longbraids would speak when he was ready.

"I could tell you I have a hundred head running on your land," Longbraids said. "But you would make a liar of me when the next tally comes around. I have almost two hundred head." Now the pride was undisguised in his voice.

"Good for you," Cal said and meant it. "I tell you what. On the next tally, I'll see that your herd is turned in as one hundred head."

Longbraids shook his head, a slow, stubborn gesture. "No," he said flatly. "I pay my way."

Cal kept his face straight. He knew he had made a bad mistake. "Any way you want it," he replied.

They rode a long way in silence, Cal wondering what he could do to make up for offending Longbraids. He decided the best thing he could do was to let it lie.

He sniffed as a disagreeable, foul odor hit his nostrils. It seemed to come from the smaller butte just ahead. On each passing breeze, the odor grew stronger.

His face showed his distaste of that rancid smell. "What the hell is that rotten smell?"

"Rattlesnakes," Longbraids replied. He

thought he read skepticism in Cal's face, because he added, "It comes from one of the biggest rattlesnake dens I have ever seen. Many of our old men say the same thing, and they have travelled much farther than I. The den is on top of the butte. Many horses will not approach it."

"Let's see if these will," Cal said. "I hate the damned things."

"I know of no one who has a love for them," Longbraids answered drily.

With each forward step, the pack horse caused Cal more trouble. He finally left him behind. Troublemaker didn't seem to be bothered as much.

"This is far enough," Longbraids said, as they reached the top of the butte. Just ahead of them was a jumbled mass of boulders, showing that in some ancient time nature had gone through a great convulsion here. Everywhere Cal looked, he saw rattlesnakes sunning themselves on the rocks.

"My God," Cal said in awe. "There's a million of them."

The exaggeration brought a fleeting smile to Longbraids' lips. "Several hundred anyway."

Cal pulled out his rifle and levered a shell into the chamber. He aimed and fired and barely noticed the broken-backed agony of the rattler before seeking a new target.

Cal emptied the rifle and was starting to reload it when Longbraids said practically, "You do not have enough ammunition to even make a small dent in them."

Cal flushed as he realized how true Longbraids' words were. "I hate the damned things," he repeated in self-justification.

"If it would do any good to hate them—"
Longbraids started, then stopped.

Cal's face burned. Longbraids was pointing out the obvious; if one could do something about what distressed him, then do it; otherwise, accept it.

Cal and Longbraids spent six days riding over the D bar S lease. The ride did not begin to cover all D bar S acres. He marked down the long draws, the grass in them brushing his knees. Along their edges were wild plums, chokecherry, Juneberry and buffalo berry thickets. Even in the most savage winter storms, the cattle could find shelter in those draws.

Supplies were running low when Cal said, "Ready to go back?"

"You've seen enough?" Longbraids asked.

Cal nodded. All of this would crack Pardee's crusty face, making it break out into a grin.

Longbraids had something on his mind, and he approached it with his usual deliberation. "Each morning, I thought I would ask you if I could ride Troublemaker. Each morning—" He let a shrug finish for him.

"I thought you'd changed your mind," Cal replied. "How about this morning?" Longbraids had seen Troublemaker go through his antics each morning. He should know what he was getting into.

Longbraids wasn't wearing spurs. Cal took his off and handed them to Longbraids.

"You'll need them." Cal said succinctly. He would find out quickly just how good a rider Longbraids was. "That devil has a trick of starting to twist to the left, then whipping the opposite way, after you commit yourself. Watch out when he lands on both forehoofs and then kicks out with his back heels. That can tear you apart."

Longbraids nodded. "I watched you ride him."

Cal didn't know whether or not that was resentment in Longbraids' voice. Maybe Longbraids had to prove something to himself; that he could do anything a white man could do. Cal shrugged away the thought. This was Longbraids battle.

Cal eared Troublemaker down while Longbraids mounted. The horse made no protest. He had had so many men try to ride him that another one didn't make any difference.

Cal let go and stepped back.

Troublemaker immediately went to work. Morning after morning, it was the same thing, Cal thought. He didn't know where this horse got all of his cussedness.

Cal knew Longbraids was a good rider. Hadn't he watched him for almost a week? But Longbraids hadn't been riding Troublemaker.

Cal hadn't known Longbraids was this good. Longbraids stuck like a burr, his body blending with every motion Troublemaker made.

After several minutes, Cal thought, he's going to make it. He wasn't sure if he was happy or disappointed.

Cal put a successful stamp on Longbraids' ride too soon. Troublemaker caught Longbraids leaning one way and whipped his body in the opposite direction.

That didn't throw Longbraids, but Cal saw it coming, for Longbraids wasn't as tight in the saddle as he had been. The graceful fluid motions of his body became abrupt and jerky, and Cal knew Longbraids was now grabbing for security.

Two more bucks finished Troublemaker's job. Longbraids went off after the second one, sailing high in the air. He lit on his butt and literally bounced.

Troublemaker bucked a few more times to show his disdain, trotted off a few yards and lowered his head to the grass. Cal never had to worry about Troublemaker running off.

For the first time, Cal saw wrath twist Longbraids' face. That stoical mask had been shattered.

"You goddamn horse," Longbraids said passionately.

Cal kept his face straight, though the restrained laughter threatened to tear him apart. "You all right?"

"I'm all right," Longbraids said stiffly. To prove it, he pushed to his feet and walked a few feet, limping slightly.

"Go ahead," he said angrily. "Laugh at me."

"Why should I?" Cal asked matter-of-factly. "I've picked myself off the ground too many times."

That mollified Longbraids somewhat, for the mask returned to his face. "I'll ride him one of these days," he growled.

"Sure you will," Cal said heartily. "You almost did this time." He wanted to add, very few men had gone as far as you did, and held the words. Longbraids might take that as flattery.

Cal didn't speak until he caught up Troublemaker and was mounted again.

Longbraids looked at him, and Cal correctly

evaluated the heat in his eyes. He spoke before Longbraids opened his mouth. "You took it all out of him for today," he said mildly.

He rode a while, and a thought kept growing in his mind. "How would you like to have him?"

Longbraids couldn't hide the flicker of surprise in his eyes.

"I mean it," Cal insisted. "I'm tired of having my ass busted every morning." Pardee would probably raise hell when he heard about this, but Cal didn't care. Troublemaker was one of the ornery ones, and after all this time, Cal hadn't chanced him. It would be a relief to get Troublemaker off his hands. "That would give you all the time you want to ride him," he finished.

Longbraids mulled the offer in his mind, and Cal thought, oh dammit. His pride and suspicions are showing. Cal felt no censure for Longbraids' attitude. If he was in the Indian's boots, he had no doubt he would feel exactly the same way.

Longbraids wanted Troublemaker. It showed in his eyes. "I cannot take him, unless I pay for him."

"Suit yourself," Cal said indifferently. "I've got another thing in mind," he said after a few minutes silence. "We need hands. I can offer you thirty dollars a month." He didn't expect a ready acceptance. That pride and suspicion wouldn't be wiped out this easily.

"That's top hand wages," Longbraids said after long thought.

"I wouldn't offer it unless I figured you can earn it."

As far as Cal was concerned, Longbraids had already proven he was worth those wages. It would be invaluable to the D bar S to have a man around who knew every inch of the lease. If Longbraids didn't have the usual skills of a top hand, Cal figured he could acquire them.

Cal waited so long for Longbraids' reply that his impatience finally got the better of him. "If you're thinking my offer is charity, get it out of your head," he said bluntly. "The D bar S doesn't throw its money away." He almost smiled. He was going to hit Pardee with two new innovations; he was giving away a horse, and he was hiring an Indian at top wages. Pardee would raised a lot of hell over at least one.

"Make up your mind," Cal said. This time, there was a snap to his tone.

He couldn't believe what he saw. That stolid mask was breaking up.

"I could pay for Troublemaker out of my wages," Longbraids said.

"Why not?" Cal replied. He felt good inside, sort of light hearted and happy.

Chapter Six

CAL'S FROWN DEEPENED as he crossed the hotel lobby. He couldn't see Hale's face, for his back was turned, but he could say positively Hale was doing fine. Hale's frequent laughter attested to that. He was drooped over the desk, claiming all of Ellie's attention. She obviously didn't mind at all, because each time Hale laughed, her gay peals rang out also.

Hale did too well with apologies to Ellie, Cal thought sourly, too damned good. Cal hadn't seen Ellie for over a week, but she had rarely been out of his mind. She was even more attractive than he recalled. Of course, he hadn't seen her laughing; that made all the difference in the world.

"Looks like you forgave him," Cal said as he reached the desk. His tone was sharper than he intended.

Ellie wouldn't quite look at him. "Why shouldn't I?" she asked lightly. "You know, you were right. He didn't mean what he said at all."

Hale's grin mocked Cal, but he didn't say anything.

"It sure makes me feel good to hear that," Cal said sardonically. He was going at this all wrong, and he knew it, but his tongue was running away with him. He thought of the scene he had interrupted, of their heads together as they laughed. By contrast he knew what a sorry picture he presented. He better change the subject in a hurry.

"How are the ribs?" he asked abruptly.

Hale slapped his side, though Cal noticed there wasn't too much force in the blow. "Better than new," Hale said. "I've been following the Doc's orders. Haven't I, Ellie?"

There was something shared between them, for her grin had a gamin like quality. "I'd say you have, Hale."

On first name basis already, Cal groaned. That boy made good time once he got started.

"I'll see you later, Ellie," Hale said and turned towards the door.

"Just a damned minute," Cal said angrily. He was full of news about the lease, and Hale wasn't going to give him a chance to talk.

"Tell me about it later," Hale said. "My pigeons are gathering. I don't want to keep them waiting."

Cal could have stopped him. He could have grabbed his shoulder and spun him around, but he knew the result of such a move. Hale would swing on him and Cal didn't want an open brawl before Ellie. He knew instinctively that Hale stood high in her eyes, and Cal sure wasn't going to do anything to tear down his own status.

Whatever Hale was doing, it pleased Ellie, for her eyes danced as she watched him disappear.

Cal turned a baffled face toward Ellie. "What's this all about?" he demanded.

She looked at Cal, and that soft, small smile made her mouth more desirable. "He's the talk of the town," she murmured. "Everybody knows Hale Decker."

"Why?" Cal demanded heatedly. "Has he been in more trouble?"

The question filled Ellie with indignation. "Why do you say that? Hale told me you're always on his back. The ones he's been playing with are in trouble."

"Oh, my God," Cal exploded. "He's been playing poker again."

She nodded, her face solemn. "Ever since you left. He's broken up game after game. He was in a hurry because there's another big game tonight."

Cal wanted to beat his fist against the desk out of sheer frustration. He wasn't really surprised to hear this. Hale was a gambler at heart, always heading for a game whenever he had the opportunity. Cal had witnessed streaks where Hale seemed unbeatable. He admitted Hale was good. Hale knew every percentage in the deck and he possessed an uncanny instinct that told him when to stay in or get out. Just the same, luck played a large part in a poker player's success, and eventually that luck ran out.

"The damned fool," Cal said. "I've seen this before. His luck will turn, and he'll wind up by losing as usual."

Ellie's eyes were stubborn. "Maybe not this time. Just before you came in, he told me that he's better than two thousand dollars ahead."

Cal whistled. That luck had carried Hale farther than Cal had ever seen it do before. Just the same he knew the ultimate outcome. He had to make Hale quit while he was ahead.

"Where's he playing?" Cal asked quietly.

Ellie read the determination in his voice and asked, "Why?"

"I'm going to knock a little sense into his head,"

Cal said grimly. He was disappointed in Ellie. By her words and manner, she backed what Hale was doing all the way. Maybe the amount of money Hale said he won had addled her brains, for most of the women Cal knew had a deep and abiding horror of gambling. Cal refused to excuse her because of her youth. Even if she hadn't been through a gambler's ups and downs, she should know that card luck had a reverse side; all black.

"Why can't you leave him alone?" Ellie flared. "He's old enough to make his own decisions."

Cal stared coldly at her. Hale had used that damned charm of his well, and he'd had enough time to completly blind her.

"Where's he playing?" he asked again.

That tough, little chin set, and Cal sighed. "You might as well tell me. This town isn't big enough that I can't find the game."

She locked eyes with him for a long moment, then gave way. "At Wakeman's saloon," she said in a low voice. "Hale won't appreciate you breaking into his game."

Cal grinned bleakly. "Probably not." He walked out of the lobby. Dammit! He hadn't asked Ellie for directions. But hadn't he told Ellie the town wasn't so big that he couldn't find something in it?

He passed a restaurant, and the rumbling in his belly reminded him he was hungry. He was sorry he'd stopped in before the third bite. The food was bad.

Cal dawdled over his second cup of coffee, debating upon the best way to confront Hale. He sighed as he finished the cup. There was no simple way.

Wakeman's sat at the far end of the street. Cal

noticed the place was doing a pretty good business as he walked inside. He soon amended that observation. The place was crowded, but it wasn't doing a great bar business. There was a triple ring of spectators around a table in the back of the room. With his height, Cal could see over most of the heads. Hale was at that table, his face as blank as though it was carved from stone. By the stacks of chips before him, Hale's winning streak was still going strong. Cal could break into the game now but decided against interfering until he cooled down.

Cal walked to the bar and ordered a drink. The bartender, a lanky, horse-faced man, made it plain that his interest was solely in the poker game. His manner said he resented even the short time it took to serve Cal.

He started away, and Cal checked him. "Hold it," he ordered. At the scowl sweeping the lanky one's face, Cal said, "That's my brother in the game. Hale Decker."

The bartender's entire attitude immediately changed. "Hale Decker is your brother?" His face brightened at Cal's nod. That relationship gave Cal special standing.

"Have another one," the bartender said, pushing the bottle toward Cal. "It's on the house."

"I haven't finished the first one yet," Cal said drily. At least, he had gained something. The bartender was willing to give him a few moments. "How's he doing?" he asked.

A look of awe touched the bartender's face. "Man, I never saw anything like this. He can't do anything wrong for doing it right. Players have heard about his streak of luck and are drifting in from all over from Minnesota and South Dakota. They've got to find out if they can break Hale's luck."

Cal didn't let his uneasiness show. It was going to be difficult to get Hale away from this game. Whatever it would take, talk or even force, Cal was determined to act.

"Wakeman even sat in tonight," the bartender said. "He's watched Hale for seven nights and he couldn't stand it any longer." The bartender chuckled at a memory. "You'd think Wakeman should know better than to smash his head against a winning streak."

Cal's eyes darkened. "Wakeman intends to stop Hale one way or another," he said significantly.

It took the bartender a moment to digest Cal's remark. "You're thinking wrong, Mister, if you think Wakeman has to use crooked cards. I've worked for him ten years, and there isn't a dishonest bone in his body. He'd have thrown a card shark out of here long before now." He shook his head, his face puzzled. "What's a damned gambler trying to do? Prove to himself or to others, that he's a better player than they are."

Cal nodded his head in agreement. Every man had a competitive streak in him about one thing or another.

Cal finished his drink, refused another, and said, "I want to talk to Hale."

The bartender chuckled agian. "Better hadn't take too long. He won't appreciate your interfering in his game."

Cal let a nod answer for him. How right that bartender was. Cal felt tight inside. He doubted he could get by using force on Hale. Judging by the bartender's admiration of Hale, Cal would find himself not only up against Hale but everybody in the saloon as well. He abandoned the idea of dragging Hale out of here. It would have to be done by talk.

He walked over to the table, where rings of onlookers were packed tightly about it. Cal could elbow his way through, but that wouldn't be wise, either.

"Hale's brother," he explained. "I've got to talk to him."

Hale's brother was a magic phrase, he thought sourly. Men willingly parted to give him passage. A few of them slapped him on the shoulder as he passed. His sourness grew. How their positions had been reversed! Before now, Cal was looked up to because he was the older brother. Now a deck of cards had made Hale the big man. And you're jealous too because of Ellie, Cal accused himself.

Cal reached the table just as Hale raked in another pot. It was a big one. Hale used both hands to pull the chips to his side of the table. His expression didn't change. He treated his winnings with no show of elation. One thing Cal could say for his brother, Hale wasn't a gloating winner.

Cal tapped Hale on the shoulder, and Hale looked up.

"You again?" Hale said. "I told you I'd talk to you later."

"Now," Cal insisted.

Hale eyed him, clearly reading the purpose in his brother's eyes and tone. He frowned but said, "Deal me out of this hand. My brother's got something all-fired important to tell me."

Cal saw nods run around the table and heard a

couple of assenting grunts. There was no open resentment in their faces at Hale's missing a hand, but just let Cal try to drag him away from his table while he was a winner. Everybody at the table would leave hoof marks all over Cal.

Hale led the way to an empty table and sat down. "Dammit, Cal," he said heatedly. "What the hell's the matter with you? You trying to jinx my winning streak?"

Cal snorted. "How many times have I heard you brag there isn't a superstitious bone in your body?"

That made Hale grin. "There isn't. But why take chances? I don't point a pistol at my head and keep pulling the trigger to be sure that every chamber is empty. Besides, you know what Pa said about something like this. When you've got luck in your hands, twist its tail hard."

"He also said a smart man knew when to buy and when to sell. You'd be smart to cash in now," Cal said levelly. "From what Ellie told me, you're way ahead."

He saw the gleam in Hale's eyes. The gambling fever was burning hot, and Cal knew Hale wouldn't listen to anything he might say now.

"Cash in now?" he hooted. "Are you crazy. Even if I wanted to get out, the other players would strip off my hide. Did you ever see a winner try to leave a table of losers?"

Cal almost nodded, but he didn't dare give Hale encouragement of any kind.

"I could take you out of here," Cal said flatly.

Hale threw back his head and laughed. "If you try it, you're a bigger damn fool than I think you are. Look at that table."

Cal glanced at the table. Every face was turned toward them. They hadn't gone on playing without Hale; they were waiting for him to return to the game.

Hale grinned. "All I have to do is to let out one squawk and they'll be on you like a pack of hungry wolves. Can you handle all of them?"

Cal was beaten and knew it. Despite the prodding of his temper, he knew what would happen to him if he tried to make Hale leave the game. He writhed inwardly. Hale wasn't worth taking a beating for.

"All right," Cal said passionately. "You go ahead your way. But Pa will be here in a few days. Just let him find you hanging around—"

He didn't bother to finish his threat. It wasn't fazing Hale in the least.

"See you around, brother," Hale said as he stood and sauntered back to the table.

Seething with fury, Cal headed back to take that drink the bartender had offered. Maybe it would help him to cool down.

Chapter Seven

CAL RETURNED TO the hotel and walked up to the desk. At the moment he was thoroughly disgusted with Hale, and he didn't want to share a room or even talk to him.

Ellie was on the desk, and her eyes widened at Cal's request for another room.

"No trouble," he explained irritably. "I just need a little more space."

"Did you see Hale?"

"I saw him." Cal didn't mean to be so abrupt. "Is he all right?"

There was a breathless little catch in her tone. Cal stared morosely at her. Right now, she too was caught up in the glamour of Hale's winning. It was all she could see. That will change, Cal thought.

He softened his voice. "From what I saw, he's doing all right." He managed to smile, and it was almost true. "Looks like he's winning half the town." He ached at the warm, happy radiance flooding her face.

Ellie's eyes were far away, and Cal prodded her, "About that room?" he said.

She blushed and asked, "Would the one next to Hale's room be all right?"

"Sure." Cal didn't want her thinking there was

an open break between him and Hale when it was just a little difference of opinion between them.

Cal took his key and climbed the stairs. He unlocked the door, tugged off his boots and stretched out on the bed, his hands locked behind his head. He stared blankly at the ceiling. All right, Ellie, he thought. How are you going to feel toward Hale when he comes dragging in with his tail beaten off? He grimaced at the thought. There was that damned spite again. A restlessness surged through him. Dammit, Pardee. Will you ever get here?

Cal made his inquiries at the railroad station the following morning. The station master said no cattle train was expected, though he thought one might be coming in tomorrow. "But I don't know who's shipping."

Oh God, Cal thought as he turned away. I hope it's the D bar S.

Hale was just starting up the stairs when Cal returned to the hotel.

Cal hailed him down and caught up with him. He had never seen Hale look any worse. His eyes were hollow, his face drawn, and he looked as though he was literally out on his feet.

"They took you," Cal said sardonically.

Hale grinned wanly. "Is that what you're hoping for? Hell, I can't remember when I last closed my eyes." He took a deep breath as though he was debating upon saying something. "Cal, the game just broke up. I took Wakeman for everything he had."

Cal stared incredulously at his brother. "You mean you won that saloon?"

"I sure did." Hale's grin drove some of the haggardness from his face.

Cal whistled. This was the biggest winning streak Hale had ever known. "What in the hell are you going to do with a saloon?"

Cal was stunned by a thought. "My God, you don't intend to be a saloon keeper?"

Hale yawned and shook his head. "Naw," he disclaimed. "Wakeman's going to run it for me. I gave him seventy-five percent of it back." He frowned as the severity of Cal's expression increased. "I don't give a damn what you say. I never had any intention of spending my life nursing a damned cow. This'll give me an income that I don't have to kiss anybody's ass for."

Cal didn't let his shock show. What Hale was saying was pure heresy. The Deckers were born cattlemen and died cattlemen. Cal was glad Pardee wasn't here to hear this.

"I guess that took most of your money," he said quietly.

"I said I gave most of the saloon back," Hale said. "Not my money. After I bankrolled Wakeman, I had most of it left. There's another big game tonight." He yawned. "I've got to get some sleep."

Hale started to go, and Cal touched him on the shoulder, stopping him. "There's a cattle train coming in tomorrow. It's about time for Pardee to be here. You'll meet the train won't you?"

"Depends on how long the game lasts," Hale said and climbed the stairs.

Cal watched him until he was out of sight. Pardee would rip the doors off of hell, if Hale wasn't at the station. Cal slowly shook his head. He would hate to have to be the one to tell Pardee that Hale thought his gambling was more important than the cattle. It wasn't that Pardee disapproved totally of gambling. He liked to sit in a game now and then as well as the next man, but he would never make it his vocation.

Cal's face was concerned as he followed Hale up the stairs. He passed the door of Hale's room without stopping. If Hale wasn't already asleep, he wouldn't want to talk. Again Cal felt a small stab of envy. He couldn't say he resented Hale too much for wanting to cut the umbilical cord. Wakeman's saloon would definitely give him an income, bringing its accompanying degree of security. Maybe it wouldn't turn out like Hale thought. If the saloon went broke, then Hale's income would be cut off.

"Damn," Cal said disgustedly to himself. "You are a spiteful bastard."

The D bar S cattle did come in the following day and Cal was at the stockyards to meet the train. He didn't expect all the cattle to be on this train; it would take several more trains to transfer them to South Dakota, but Cal could bet that Pardee would be with the first bunch.

His face brightened as he saw the short stocky figure limp down the car steps. The limp came from a broken leg in a bad fall from a horse. The bone never healed properly, Cal knew there were times it gave his father pure hell, but he also knew no one better be foolish enough to be solicitous about the leg. Pardee would take his head off.

"Pa," Cal said. He tried to keep the greeting as casual as though he had just seen Pardee this morning. Pardee also didn't like a display of emotion.

"Cal," Pardee replied and wrung Cal's hand. He was almost a head shorter than Cal and was thickening about the waist. That grizzled face was as tough as a granite knob, and it was deeply lined and creased. Although Pardee was only fifty years old, he had known a lot of hard living.

"How'd the cattle come through?" Cal asked. That was the question Pardee wanted to hear. He didn't want any damned nonsense about how he had stood the trip.

"Maybe as good as could be expected," Pardee grunted. "We got some cattle down. We've got to get them out of those stinking cars. Jesus Christ," he said explosively. "What a way to move cattle."

Cal wisely held his tongue. Pardee would have been happier if he had driven the cattle all the way from Texas to South Dakota.

Pardee looked around. "Where's Hale?"

Cal won a bet he had made with himself. He had bet that Pardee's first words would be, "Where's Hale?"

"He's busy, Pa. He'll be along later." God forgive him for that lie. He knew Pardee wouldn't.

"Busy," Pardee snorted. "What have you two had to do but lie around on your butts all this time?"

Cal kept his face stolid. That was Pardee, making a judgment before he had all the facts.

"I've ridden all over the lease," Cal said quietly.

Pardee looked sharply at him. Cal didn't expect an apology; to Pardee, that was a waste of time.

"What do you think?" Pardee asked.

"Pa, you wouldn't believe it," Cal replied. "You couldn't pick better grass if you went to

Heaven and had your choice of the grazing there." Cal chuckled. "Not that you'll ever have that opportunity."

"You're turning into a real funny man," Pardee said sourly, but his face brightened at Cal's report, and some of the tension seemed to slip away from him. "Let's see about getting the cattle unloaded."

Cal hid his relief. For the moment he had taken Pardee's attention off of Hale.

Cal greeted old friends. Pardee had brought most of the crew with him, and it was a pleasure to see them again. But he looked at three of them with a jaundiced eye. He had hoped Deke Briscoe and his two sons would decide to stay in Texas. If Cal had his way, he would have gotten rid of Briscoe a long time ago. But Briscoe had once saved Pardee's life in a stampede, and Pardee never forgot that. As long as he was alive and had jobs to pass around, Briscoe and his sons would never be without one.

"Deke," Cal murmured. He didn't offer to shake hands with him.

Briscoe caught the ommission, for his eyes were malicious. "Well Dent, Jude," he said to his sons, standing beside him. "Look what we got here."

"He'll make sore eyes worse," Jude said and spit an amber stream of tobacco juice near Cal's boot. He didn't dare come any closer. That was insult enough and Dent's chuckle didn't cool the heat building up in Cal.

The three Briscoes came out of the same mold. Except for the age discrepancy, there was little difference in the three. They were lanky men, standing loose, looking almost disjointed. Their faces had a tight pinched look and they never looked quite clean. Dent and Jude were barely adequate hands, doing just enough to keep Pardee off of their backs, and Deke Briscoe was a miserable cook. Damn Pardee and his misplaced sense of obligation.

"Pardee wants to get the cattle off," Cal said. Neither of the three Briscoes made any effort to move, and Cal snapped, "Now."

"Sounds like we're back home," Dent said and grinned at his brother.

Cal whirled on his heel, avoiding further words. He had jumped on them before, and Pardee always intervened on the Briscoes' side.

Cal was steaming as he helped with the unloading. He hoped one of these days Pardee would get smart and pay the Briscoes off. But he shook his head. So far, that was a futile hope.

The horses, ten to a hand, shipped well, but the cattle were in worse shape. They were gaunt, their ribs standing out starkly from the prolonged period of semi-starvation. They came haltingly down the chutes, bawling pitiously.

Cal shook his head as he looked into the shipping cars after the cattle were out. In each car were a few dead animals, and some hopelessly crippled, they would have to be destroyed. Pardee had every right to those deep, unhappy lines in this face. He hated losing an animal to disease, the brutality of nature, or to a predator. Maybe those lines would be erased, or at least softened when he saw the grass that was ahead of them.

The cattle milled cheerlessly around in the pens after they were unloaded, filling the air with dust stirred up by their hoofs.

Cal found Pardee and gestured at the nearby surrounding hills. "Good grass up there. We can hold them there until they get stronger."

Pardee blew out a hard breath. "Well, that's something. I thought this goddamned trip would never end. Lead the way, Cal." He jerked off his hat and waved it at his riders. "Move them out," he bawled.

Cal grinned. Every man in the state could have heard Pardee. He could say one thing for a cattleman's life; it developed his lungs.

"Deke," Pardee bellowed at Briscoe and beckoned him over. "Get the cook wagon unloaded. I want supper and hot coffee before dark."

"I can't do it by myself," Briscoe complained.

Cal surveyed him coldly. Briscoe was pushing his luck.

"You got Dent and Jude, don't you?" Pardee asked coldly.

Pardee sighed as he watched Briscoe walk away. "Sometimes, he rasps me good."

Good, Cal exalted. Briscoe's hold on Pardee was getting more and more flimsy.

Pardee destroyed the thought by adding, "Then I remember what he did for me."

Cal wanted to howl his protest, but kept his mouth shut. Bitter experience had taught him how useless it was to argue when his father's mind was made up.

Cal picked a horse out of the remuda and saddled. He felt Pardee's hard, inquisitive eyes on him and turned his head away. He didn't want to explain anything now, even though he knew he was merely postponing the inevitable. His father would have to be told about Longbraids and Troublemaker, and Hale.

Cal led the way, the bawling cattle pushing behind him. He wanted to yell at the constant din, shut up, will you? A couple of miles is all you have to go.

The grass began to thicken but the cattle still fought being pushed farther. The riders behind them worked hard to keep them going, and Cal knew they were wondering what in the hell was he doing. Cal wanted to reach the little bowl just a little way ahead; the grass was even better there. Those starved animals would find themselves in paradise, and spend most of the night filling their empty bellies.

The first wave of cattle stopped when they hit the bowl. Only the pressure of the cattle behind them shoved them on.

"I thought you were taking us to Canada," Pardee growled when he caught up to Cal.

Cal gave him a pained grin. Pardee was complaining about a two mile drive. This was one of those times when nothing pleased Pardee.

"I better see what's happening to the chuck wagon," Cal said and turned back. He knew this trip wasn't necessary, but it did postpone telling Pardee about Troublemaker and Longbraids. Pardee's yell didn't stop Cal.

Cal rode a mile before he saw the chuck wagon coming, the stove cart behind it. The cart was mounted on two wheels, and its short tongue was fastened to the wagon axle by a stout chain. The chain with its big hook was pulled up tight and bolted to the wagon. Even reckless driving over rough ground couldn't lose that cart. Briscoe and his two sons sat on the wagon seat, and Briscoe yelled warthfully at Cal, "Goddammit, I'm coming. Did you expect me to fly?"

Cal's lips thinned, but he made no answer. One

of these days, he was going to cram some of that smart talk down Briscoe's throat.

He whirled and rode back to Pardee. "It's coming," he announced.

Pardee nodded his acknowledgement. His eyes were riveted on the grazing cattle. He looked more at peace than Cal had seen him in a long time.

"I hired a new hand," Cal said casually. "A man named Joe Longbraids."

Pardee looked at him, frowning slightly. "Longbraids," he mused. "Damned odd name." His eyes widened. "Don't tell me he's a damned Indian."

Cal nodded. "Three-quarters Sioux." He braced himself. The storm was gathering in Pardee's face. "He led me all over the lease. Knows every foot of it. He should since he was born and raised here. Dammit, Pardee, we need a man who knows where he is."

Pardee considered that, and the storm in his face lessened. "Maybe," he said reluctantly. "What'd you offer him?"

"Thirty dollars a month!" As the storm begun again Cal quickly added, "He'll be worth every cent of it. If he isn't take it out of my pocket."

"By God, he better be worth it," Pardee grumbled.

Cal drew a careful breath. He might as well tell Pardee about Troublemaker and get it over with all at once. He stared ahead as he said, "I gave him Troublemaker."

"You gave away a D bar S horse," Pardee exploded. "Who the hell do you think you are—"

Cal cut him short. "I was the only one in the outfit who could ride him, Pa. I got sick and tired of that damned hammerhead raising hell every morning. What good was Troublemaker, if nobody else could ride him?"

Pardee squinted at his son. "Are you telling me this Indian can ride him?"

Cal told a calculated lie. "He can," he said stoutly. Longbraids hadn't been able to ride Troublemaker the last time Cal had seen him, but he had a strong conviction that Longbraids would. Make it soon, Joe, Cal prayed.

"If he can fork that horse, maybe your Indian isn't worthless," Pardee grumbled. "I'll keep a close eye on him," he warned.

"Sure," Cal said, expecting that of Pardee. He turned his head at the rumble of wheels. "Chuck wagon's coming."

"It took Briscoe long enough," Pardee snapped. "Tell him I want some coffee."

Cal rode up to the wagon and said, "Pardee wants coffee now." At the indignation forming in Briscoe's face, he said coldly, "You go tell him you just got here."

The thought of confronting Pardee shut Briscoe up.

Cal sat in his saddle watching Briscoe build his fire, then drag out a new one hundred pound sack of Arbuckle's whole coffee beans from the long chuck box built across the rear of the wagon. When the door to the box was dropped, it was turned into a convenient work table.

Briscoe never stopped muttering as he poured some of the beans into the flat-sided coffee grinder bolted to the side of the wagon. As he ground the beans, he raised his voice so it could be heard above the noise of the grinding. Cal heard him complaining, "Not a goddamned minute anymore for a man to catch his breath." He looked up at Cal and said, "I'm hurrying, ain't I? You don't have to sit and watch me."

"I'm waiting to take it over to Pardee," Cal said coldly.

It was a good twenty minutes before the coffee was ready. Briscoe handed Cal a cup of coffee, and Cal didn't miss the malicious glint in his eyes. He had filled the cup to the brim, knowing that Cal couldn't help but spill some of it before he reached Pardee.

Cal, refusing to give Briscoe any satisfaction, didn't say a word, but turned and rode slowly, holding the cup carefully. Despite all his care, some of the contents sloshed over onto his leg. He swore in sudden rage. That goddamned coffee was boiling hot and burnt through his pants leg.

Cal finished the short ride without spilling anymore coffee and wordlessly handed Pardee the cup.

Pardee looked sourly at it. "A half cup. What's he trying to do—ration me?"

"I didn't ask him," Cal said shortly. He could report the too filled cup, but that would be interpreted as tattletelling. All he could do was to continue to hope that Briscoe's bad disposition would spill over and touch Pardee one of these days.

Pardee took a swallow of the coffee, and his face turned violent. He spewed out the coffee, spraying it before him.

For a moment, Cal thought the coffee was too hot, but the ride here should have cooled it.

"Worst goddamned coffee I ever tasted," Pardee spat. "Tastes just like a cup of warmed over horse piss."

Cal was beginning to enjoy this. "I wouldn't

know. Never tasted horse piss. Briscoe's your man."

Pardee glared at Cal, then threw down his cup. His face was a thundercloud and Cal hoped Pardee's wrath would burst and flood Briscoe.

Instead Pardee said in a voice that trembled with anger. "Where's Hale?"

Cal groaned. He should have known that Pardee wouldn't have forgotten about Hale. "Pa, I don't know. I guess he just got tied up."

"Tied up hell," Pardee raved. "What did he do? Find some doxie in town?"

Cal sighed. It might as well come out now. He couldn't protect Hale any longer. "Pa, I think he's in a poker game." He saw the thundercloud build up to horrendous proportions on Pardee's face.

"A damned poker game," Pardee said furiously. "He thinks it's so damned important that he missed the unloading."

Cal wanted to turn some of that wrath away from Hale. "Pa," he said earnestly. "He's doing real well. The whole town's talking about his winning." He rushed on, trying to forstall Pardee's burst of anger. "Pa, didn't you always tell him when you're on a winning streak to ride it to the end."

That momentarily set Pardee back. He blinked several times. But he recovered his anger quickly. "Not when he had his own business to attend to. You know where he is?" At Cal's weak nod, he said, "Let's go and get him."

Cal's face was concerned as he rode beside Pardee. Maybe when his father found out the magnitude of Hale's winning, it would cool him off.

Chapter Eight

CAL THOUGHT IT best to stop at the hotel, hoping Hale was still there. He shuddered at the thought of the confrontation between Hale and Pardee.

Ellie was behind the desk, and Cal said. "Ellie, this is my father, Pardee Decker. Is Hale here?"

Ellie extended a hand to Pardee, giving him her best smile. "I'm happy, sir, to meet Hale's father."

Pardee's cold face didn't melt. "I want to talk to Hale."

Ellie's entire manner changed. She had a crust of her own, and Pardee's attitude brought it out. "I don't know where he is," she snapped.

Two pieces of flint were striking against each other, and already the sparks were flying.

Cal stepped hastily in between them. He knew that Ellie was trying to protect Hale. "Ellie, it's important. The cattle just came in. Is Hale at Wakeman's?"

She bit her lower lip. Cal thought she was going to refuse to answer, but she nodded reluctantly.

"Thanks, Ellie," Cal said softly and led Pardee out of the lobby. Her eyes hadn't softened in the least; she wasn't forgiving Pardee for his roughness. Neither of them had shown the slightest intention of saying they were happy to know each other.

"Hale interested in that doxie?" Pardee asked when they got outside.

"Don't call her that," Cal flared. "She's a respectable girl, doing her best to make a success out of that hotel."

Pardee gave him a long, hard look, then shouted, "So, she's got you hooked too. I could expect something like this from Hale, but I thought you had better sense."

"Don't say any more," Cal snapped. Crossing Pardee wasn't going to improve his mood, but Cal wasn't going to be pushed into the position of having to defend Ellie. Pardee had seen her; he should know she wasn't the kind of a girl he was suggesting.

Pardee didn't try to push it farther. A strained silence enveloped both of them by the time they stepped into Wakeman's.

Cal looked around him. The place was doing a rushing business. If anything, it was far busier than the other time he had been here. The bar was lined. A solid mass of men surrounded a table. Cal couldn't help thinking of the cut Hale was getting out of this night's business.

"I don't see him," Pardee growled.

Cal pointed at the men surrounding the table. He couldn't see the players, but was pretty certain that was where Hale would be.

"Over there, Pa," he said.

Cal was tall enough to see over the heads of most of the watchers as he approached the table. Hale was here all right. It seemed that fabulous streak of luck hadn't lessened. Hale looked as though he was building a solid wall of poker chips.

Pardee didn't have the advantage of Cal's height, and for a moment didn't see Hale. He lifted himself on his toes, caught sight of Hale, and nodded. His face was grim.

He plowed straight ahead, Shoving men out of his way.

Cal wanted to yell at him to take it easy, but it was too late. Pardee already had stepped, literally and figuratively, on too many toes. Cal heard the cuss words thrown after Pardee. Cal sighed and followed in his wake.

"Hale," Pardee thundered as he reached the table.

Hale looked up. No guilt or fear showed on his face. "Hello, Pa." He gestured at the stacks of chips before him. "I'm doing all right."

Pardee's voice lowered, and Cal thought it sounded more ominous. "The cattle got in today."

Hale shrugged. "I thought they had. You're here, aren't you?"

Pardee's jaw sagged, and for a moment he was speechless. Then his face tightened, and he said accusingly, "You weren't there to help."

Hale grinned. "I was busy. Besides, you got along all right, didn't you?"

Cal groaned at the audacity of the words. Couldn't Hale see the mood Pardee was in? Was he deliberately trying to bait Pardee?

Pardee looked shocked, then gathered his scattered thoughts. "Come on," he roared. "We're getting out of here."

Hale was still grinning, though the smile was fading fast. "Can't, Pa. I'm ahead." He waved at the men around the table. "They wouldn't like it."

The growl running around the table, confirmed Hale's statement.

Pardee was livid. "Don't talk back to me," he shouted. "Stand up."

Hale's eyes narrowed as he bunched the cards he held and laid them on the table. "Sure," he replied quietly. He stood and added, "But it won't change anything. I'm not leaving until I'm ready."

The blood congesting in Pardee's face made it look purple. "Don't you talk back to me," he said, his voice shaking with anger. His hand lashed out and he slapped Hale across the mouth.

Cal heard the collective suck of breath run around the table. He felt sick inside. Even if he had moved the instant it happened, he couldn't have stopped Hale's reaction.

Hale hit Pardee full on the jaw, and splat of the blow made an ugly sound in the suddenly hushed room.

Hale would probably never throw a better punch. Pardee staggered backwards, his arms flailing to retain his balance. He went down hard, his head striking against the floor.

He wasn't out, for his eyes still stared vaguely about him, and his hands clutched spasmodically at the floor.

Cal bent over him. He lifted Pardee's head to ease his labored breathing. His eyes were hot and bitter as he looked at Hale.

"You poor damned fool," he said slowly.

Hale's face was white and he looked utterly miserable. Pardee's slap had broken skin at the corner of a lip, and a trickle of blood ran down Hale's chin.

"Cal," he said pleadingly. "I didn't mean to do

that. But he hurt me. I saw red and before I knew it, I hit back."

Under the sting of the slap and the embarrassment of all those watching eyes, Hale had lashed out instinctively. Cal could understand, but would Pardee?

He looked down at Pardee. His eyes were clearing, Even at his age, Pardee was still a damned good man. Cal had seen him get up a half-dozen times after having been knocked down, and Pardee was wilder and tougher each time. Cal would hate to be in Hale's boots. He didn't think Hale would try to hit Pardee again, but would Pardee stop? That was the big question, and in some way Cal had to prevent it from happening.

"You need any help, Hale?" somebody asked.

Hale whirled, and his face was a twisted, savage mask. "You stay out of this," he yelled. "I'll knock the sonuvabitch's head off who tries to interfere."

Cal was grateful for that. It would keep this from turning into a brawl, because of Hale's standing with these men.

"Let go of me," Pardee said, pushing "I'm all right."

He struggled to his feet, fighting his limber legs. Cal afraid Pardee would rush Hale, was ready to step in between them.

"Let's go, Cal," Pardee said. His voice was dead.

"Pa," Hale cried. "I didn't mean to do that."

Pardee whirled on Hale, and Cal expected to see his face livid with rage, but it had no more life than his voice.

"Keep away from me," Pardee said. His voice

was changing; it was beginning to quiver with passion. "I don't ever want to see you again."

Cal watched Hale's face turn sick and white. He shook his head at Hale, then followed Pardee out of the saloon.

They walked back to the horses, almost reaching them before Pardee spoke. "I suppose you don't approve of what I did."

"No," Cal snapped. "He hit you because you stung him good. You saw his face. It made him sick. What else did you expect him to do?"

"He's my son," Pardee said hotly. "He hit me in front of all of those people."

"After you slapped him in front of all of those people," Cal said wearily.

"I've still got the right do discipline my sons, if I see it's needed."

"You had the right," Cal corrected him, "up to an age. Hale's grown up now."

"I could have whipped him," Pardee said stubbornly. "But I didn't want all those strangers seeing me and Hale clawing at each other like two strange tomcats."

Thank God Pardee had had enough pride to want to avoid that bitter spectacle. Maybe Pardee could have whipped Hale and maybe he couldn't. But if it came down to fist work, Cal felt quite sure everybody in the room would have been behind Hale. Cal grimaced at the thought of the beating he and Pardee would have taken. He thought morosely; he had always considered the Decker family a tight little unit. Now that the little unit was split wide open.

"It almost killed me when your Ma died," Pardee said in a voice so low that Cal barely caught it.

"This hurts almost as bad."

Cal felt a renewed surge of hope. If Pardee felt that way, then perhaps the split could be mended. All that was needed was a little honest talk.

"Pa, Hale wouldn't want a split between you and him. I'll go get him, and we'll talk."

Cal couldn't believe his eyes. Fury had seized Pardee's face again. "After him knocking me down before all those people, you think I could take him back?" Pardee worked himself into a higher rage. "I'll be damned, if I will," he shouted. "Let him wear out his ass playing poker until he goes broke. Then, he'll come crawling back quick enough."

The shock of the words stopped Cal short, and he let Pardee plow doggedly ahead. The vengeful old bastard! Pardee wanted to see Hale beg; he wanted to grind Hale's nose into this mess. Cal felt sick inside. He knew Hale's pride. Hale would never beg for a damned thing. The sickness mingled with rage. If there was only some way he could pound some sense into Pardee's head. Cal let go of the thought. Nothing was going to make Pardee change his mind.

Pardee reached his horse and mounted. He turned his head and yelled at Cal, "Are you coming or not? We've got cattle on our hands."

Cal picked up his stride. This wasn't a family unit any more. It carried the same name, but that was all. Oh, damn your winning streak, Hale.

Chapter Nine

OVER A WEEK passed before all of the D bar S cattle arrived. One train after another rolled up to the stockyards and unloaded, and a new semi-starved herd would be turned out to fatten themselves on the good grass outside of Evarts. Cal didn't see Hale again and for the most part was too busy to even think much about him. He didn't expect to see Hale come around, even if he went broke as Pardee hoped. Hale could be reduced to hunting scraps in the gutter, and he would never approach Pardee. Cal cussed both of them for their stiff-necked pride.

Cal hoped Pardee would break down and say something about Hale, but again he should have known better than that. Pardee talked, but Hale was never mentioned. He had locked his younger son out of his mind. Hale no longer existed.

Pardee found Cal this morning, and he was mad. Cal wondered what had gotten him so stirred. The cattle were gaining strength daily from the lush grazing, and he could swear the first arrivals had picked up quite a few pounds.

"Do you know what that damned Indian Department told me this morning?" Pardee demanded.

"You haven't told me yet," Cal said.

Pardee glared at him before he went on. "Every head we own has to be dipped for scabies before they can be ferried across the river."

Cal nodded before he could catch himself.

"You knew about this?" Pardee said astounded.

"Well, scabies is contagious," Cal explained. "South Dakota is clean of the mites that cause it. The Department wants to make sure the range isn't infected."

"Why didn't you tell me about this before?" Pardee howled.

Cal blew out a breath. Frankly, it had slipped his mind.

"Would it have made you happier, if I hit you with this the moment you arrived. I thought you had too much else on your mind."

That mollified Pardee a little, but he still grumbled. "Dammit. There's always something to plague a man. I wanted to send the first herd over today."

But you can't, Cal could have pointed out. He held the words.

"Let's get at it," Pardee said heavily. "These goddamned regulations are going to drive me out of my mind."

You don't need any help there, Cal thought, staring at his father. You're doing a pretty good job by yourself. He felt pity for Pardee. He could swear Pardee had aged in the few days since his clash with Hale.

Evarts had two dipping vats, one a hundred and fifty feet long, the other somewhat shorter. Weaker cattle went through the short vat, for the hot swim sapped at the strength they had left. The Department had veterinarians on both sides of the vats to be sure every head was thoroughly ducked.

The water in the dips was uncomfortably warm to the touch, and the lime and sulphur solution had a nauseating stench.

Cal had watched the operation just before Pardee and the cattle arrived. The mixture turned the cattle a bluish yellow, and although it wore off in a few days, Pardee would cuss some more when he saw his cattle coming out of the dips.

The cattle were driven down a long, fenced-in lane and forced off a steel slide into the dip. Each animal leaped widly when he came to the end of the slide. Its leap carried it to the bottom of the vat, and every square inch of it was thoroughly doused in the mixture. But the veterinarians and the Department officials weren't satisfied with just one ducking. They demanded that each head be submerged several times in its swim toward the end of the vat.

Pardee's hands stood along each side of the vat above the swimming cattle. Cal didn't see the Briscoes, and he wished he had the time to go hunt them up. It was typical of the Briscoes to avoid any odious task.

"The worthless bastards," Cal muttered as he waited for the first head to pass. He held a long steel rod that had an S-shaped hook at the end of it. The down curve of the S hooked an animal's neck and pushed its head under. The up curve lifted the animal's head so that he could get his breath.

The cattle poured down the chute faster and faster until the vat was a sea of bobbing heads. It was hard and tiring work to be sure each head was ducked. Cal's arms began to ache from using the rod but he knew every one of Pardee's riders was going through the same ordeal.

"Except the Briscoes," Cal muttered, as he

shoved another head under.

No matter how hard he worked, those government officials were never satisfied. "Duck him, duck him," they yelled. "You missed that one." Their voices pounded at Cal's ears until he was sick of their orders. He was beginning to feel toward them as Pardee did. These government men were so damned officious and authoritative.

Cattle drowned in those vats. Several times Cal saw cattle go under. Despite his frantic efforts with the S-shaped hook, he couldn't get the animal's head up in time. The pressure of the oncoming waves of cattle kept the unfortunate animal under until he drowned. Pardee was swearing at his loss. Cal could hear him saying bitterly, "The goddamned regulations won't pay for this."

Cal sympathized with Pardee but there wasn't anything the Deckers could do about it; not if they wanted to lease the grass they needed.

Cal was bone-tired as the last of the first herd was driven through the vats. He was drenched from the mixture, splashed up on him by the threshing hoofs of the cattle. He smelled to high Heaven. The sickening part was, that all this would have to be done over and over until the last D bar S head went through the vat.

The dipping wasn't finished until the following morning, and Pardee asked sarcastically, "Can I cross now, Mister?"

The young official completely missed Pardee's sarcasm. "You can, Mr. Decker," he replied. "You've complied with every regulation."

By Pardee's sour expression Cal thought he was choking on the word 'regulation.'

Pardee was aghast when he first saw the ferry. He looked at the ferry, then at the expanse of muddy water it had to cross.

"Is it safe?" Pardee asked in a weak voice. He had an excessive fear of water. As a child, he had almost drowned, and he never had learned to swim.

Cal grinned. "I crossed it twice. I got over and back, didn't I?"

Pardee scowled at him. "But not with a load of cattle," he objected.

That was true, Cal admitted. But other outfits had made the same crossing Cal told him. There was no reason to think D bar S cattle couldn't go the same way.

Pen after pen with its own gate was filled with cattle, and Pardee was astounded at the total. "Goddamn floating stockyards," he said when Cal told him that five hundred head of cattle could be handled on a trip.

He tried to grin at Cal, but it didn't come off well. "It'll take another trip and most of a third to get this bunch moved over."

Cal was sorry for Pardee; he was strung tighter than new wire. Cal could tell by the way his knuckles stood out as he gripped the railing that Pardee would never draw a free breath until his boots were on solid ground.

"No sense of us going back with the ferry," Cal said casually. "The other boys can handle it."

Pardee's long, tearing sigh showed his relief. He tried to cover up this display of weakness by saying, "I guess that would work out all right."

He rode off the ferry after it landed and dismounted immediately. Cal didn't dare grin at him.

"I'll never get used to that damned boat," Pardee said crossly.

Cal wanted to say, you'd better, but he didn't.

Pardee would have to cross that river many times, if he lived long in this country.

Cal kept Duff Granger with them. Granger was a top hand with many years of service with Pardee. Age was beginning to touch him around the edges, in the seamed face and the deliberation with which he moved. But he was still a good man. He let reasoning replace the piss and vinegar of a younger man.

Cal and Granger drove the cattle off the ferry, and Cal announced, "Now, you're in the Strip." He explained what the Strip was, and Pardee and Granger were impressed with the way the railroad had simplified the handling of cattle. The cattle appreciated the good grass around them, for they immediately fell to grazing.

"Six miles wide," Pardee said in wonder. "This is what I'd call a lane. A man wouldn't have to do much worrying about his cattle scattering here. Hell, I've chased a stampede a hell of a lot farther than that." He looked at the growth of the grass in the Strip and said reflectively, "Lot of grass going to waste though."

"You're using it now, aren't you?" Cal pointed out. "The Strip adjoins our lease. We can use it when no other herds are being driven through."

Pardee was spare in his praise of anything, but his eyes gleamed. "Everything might work out all right," he said grudgingly.

Cal got so mad at Pardee that he wanted to cuss him out good. Good Lord, did anything ever please him? To keep himself from speaking and starting a fuss, he rode on ahead of the grazing cattle to keep them from wandering deeper into the Strip.

Granger joined him. He hooked a knee over the

horn and said, "I guess this is where God promises a cowboy he'll go when he dies."

Cal chuckled. Here was real appreciation. "Could be, Duff."

Granger turned his head to look at the ferry. It had already cast off and was chugging its way back toward the opposite shore. "I don't care how long it takes that ferry to bring over the rest of the cattle."

"Pardee will," Cal said flatly. But he understood what Granger meant. At the moment, nothing was pressing them. This was a pleasant interlude in the midst of too many pressure-filled hours.

The ferry returned and unloaded the second five hundred cattle, then headed back for the remainder.

"Should be about two hundred left," Granger said.

"Yep," Cal answered. "Then we start sending another bunch through the vats."

Granger groaned. That session at the dipping vats had worn him out, too. "Chuck wagon on the last ferry?" he asked.

"Should be," Cal replied. He wanted to talk to the Briscoes. When Pardee had ordered all hands to the dipping vats, that meant the Briscoes, too.

Granger looked sour at Cal's answer, and Cal asked, "Something go down wrong, Duff?"

Granger hawked and spit, his face filled with disgust. "I was thinking of another rotten meal that Briscoe'll serve." His tone picked up a plaintive note. "Why does Pardee keep him on? If he had a decent cook, this would be a pretty good outfit."

"You ask Pardee about that," Cal replied. He

wasn't going to try to explain the loyalty Pardee felt to Deke Briscoe. That was Pardee's business.

Cal was watching the unloading of the cattle, and he caught just a glimpse of a rider behind the cattle.

"I'll be damned," he said softly. "Do you see what I see?"

"I've seen cattle before," Granger said. "There's that damned chuck wagon coming off."

Cal nodded impatiently. He had seen the chuck wagon, and Briscoe was driving it down the gangplank. Behind it was the big tent wagon, and Jude and Dent were on the driver seat. Cal was going to have a few words with them, but right now something else claimed his attention.

"Duff, don't tell me you've forgotten Troublemaker."

Granger stared in disbelief. "I'll be goddamned. I should remember him. If my mind doesn't, my bruises do. For God's sake," he said in awe. "Who's that riding him?"

"Joe Longbraids," Cal said proudly. "I hired him on." All his disappointment in Longbraids faded. He had felt let down when Longbraids hadn't shown up earlier. He had even made a few inquiries in town, but no one knew where Longbraids was. Cal mentally apologized to Longbraids for thinking the Indian had just taken Troublemaker and forgotten all about the job Cal had offered him.

Cal was grinning all over his face when Longbraids rode up and joined him and Granger.

"Hello, Joe," Cal said quietly. "I was beginning to wonder where you were."

Longbraids looked as though he had been through a rough time. One side of his face was

THE RAGGED EDGE

scraped raw, and he sat stiffly in the saddle as though his bones hurt.

Longbraids came close to a grin. "This is the first day I've been able to ride him," he said proudly.

Cal could visualize all the times Longbraids had been thrown. It had taken tremendous determination to keep at it time after time.

"I knew you would," Cal said. Their eyes met and there was respect in the exchanged glance.

"Duff," Cal said, "this is Joe Longbraids. I turned Troublemaker over to him."

Granger's eyes swept over the rider and horse. "You did a job," he said. "Outside of Cal you're the first man who could handle that brute."

Longbraids nodded without speaking, but the swelling pride glowed in his face.

The chuck wagon came up and started to pass, and Cal said, "Hold it, Briscoe. I want to talk to you."

The tent wagon pulled up behind Briscoe, and Jude and Dent looked curiously at Longbraids.

"Ain't he pretty?" Jude jeered. "What the hell's he made up for?"

Cal rode over to them and said savagely, "You keep your damned mouth shut. He's a better man than either of you. He's riding Troublemaker."

A dull red burned in their faces. Both of them had tried to ride Troublemaker. After Troublemaker had bounced them off onto the ground, neither Jude nor Dent had tried it again.

Cal swept them with a final searing glance, then turned and rode up beside the chuck wagon.

"Where were you while the dipping was going on?" he asked furiously.

Briscoe looked indolently at Cal. Cal's anger

didn't faze him in the least. Briscoe turned the cud over in his mouth and spat a long stream over the wagon's wheel. "I had things to do."

"You needed Jude and Dent?" Cal fought to keep control over his rising temper.

Briscoe grinned at him. "I needed them." His indignation rose, and he said, "Did you expect me to drive both wagons? I needed Jude and Dent to drive the other wagon." Briscoe was working himself up, but Cal thought there was a false ring in it.

"You didn't need both of them," Cal said coldly.

"I needed them to help me make the necessary repairs on the wagons, didn't I?" Briscoe yelped.

Cal knew he was a damned liar. Pardee insisted upon keeping his equipment in top shape. "What repairs?" he asked.

Briscoe gestured vaguely. "Oh, you know. I had to check all the rims to be sure they were tight. And I sure didn't want a spoke coming out on me."

"Stop it," Cal said wearily. If he would let him, Briscoe could come up with a list longer than his arm. Cal leaned forward and pointed an accusing finger at Briscoe. "I'm warning you, Deke, you duck out of any more jobs, and I'll make damn sure Pardee hears about it."

He rode away, leaving Briscoe spluttering.

Pardee was there when Cal rejoined Longbraids and Granger. Cal didn't like that speculative gleam in Pardee's eyes as he looked at Longbraids.

"Joe Longbraids, Pa," he said. "I told you about hiring him."

There was no softening in Pardee's hard, impassive face. "I know who he is. Duff told me." He pointed a finger at Longbraids. "Let me tell you one thing. I expect you to earn your wages."

Cal expected Longbraids' eyes to burn. Pardee could make any comment sound like a insult. Goddammit, Cal raved silently. Couldn't Pardee see that Longbraids had pride? Pardee didn't have to worry about a man like that earning his wages.

Pardee softened the moment by saying grudgingly, "I'll say one thing. You're one hell of a rider."

Cal grinned at Longbraids. The stoic mask of Longbraids' face hadn't cracked, but Cal was sure there was warmth in Longbraids' eyes.

"What the hell are we sitting around here for?" Pardee said impatiently. "We've got cattle to move. Longbraids, Cal said you know this land. Start earning your wages. Lead the way."

Chapter Ten

AFTER THE CATTLE were turned onto the D bar S lease, there was no immediate pressure. Cal and Longbraids led Pardee around the lease. Pardee's eyes were thoughtful slits as he observed everything. Cal remembered his own wild enthusiasm the first time he had seen this piece of South Dakota. He expected Pardee to feel the same elation. My God, it had been so long since Pardee had looked at virgin grass like this. If Pardee felt anything, he didn't express it by a single word.

Cal felt a deep affection for the old hard head. Pardee had steeled himself all his life not to show weakness, and to him, voicing delight was a form of weakness.

"Pa, do you think there's enough grass so that we don't have to worry about it running out?" Cal asked teasingly.

Pardee missed the humor entirely. He weighed the question judiciously then said, "It should last, Cal."

Cal shook his head. Longbraids caught that enchange between father and son. No grin showed on that impassive face, but Cal would bet Longbraids was grinning inwardly.

Cal pointed out everything he could to get a single word of approval from Pardee. He talked about the long grass-choked ravines, and said, "Even in a bad winter, the cattle will find the ravines and drift into them. We won't have to worry about them starving, either."

"Could be," Pardee said laconically.

"Good grass," Longbraids grunted. "In summer turns brown. Just like hay. Much feed."

Cal frowned at him. Longbraids could speak English as well as he and Pardee, but Cal had noticed Longbraids often lapsed into pidgin English. Some perverse streak in Longbraids made him do this, Cal thought. Two natural streaks of stubbornness had met and clashed. Let Pardee think he was dealing with an ignorant Indian. Longbraids wasn't going to make the slightest effort to change the unfavorable impression.

Pardee sensed some criticism in Longbraids' words. He snapped, "What's wrong with that?"

"Could be bad," Longbraids grunted. He spread his hands wide. "Fire comes. Big blaze. Always comes."

Pardee stared at him in outrage. "Why goddammit," he exploded. "Do you expect me to go around worrying about everything that might happen. That could drive a man out of his mind."

He spun his horse and sank his spurs deep, heading back to the house.

"Why do you bait him?" Cal asked.

That might have been a twitch in Longbraids' lips. "He is always so positive," Longbraids said softly. "He has not yet learned that there are some things a man cannot change."

Cal nodded. Longbraids hadn't known Pardee very long, but he had evaluated him accurately.

Cal's nod gave Longbraids the courage to finish what he had in mind. "Have you ever seen a prairie fire?" he asked earnestly. "They sweep faster than a horse can run. Then the grass is gone until there is a good rain. I was only trying to point out what could happen."

Cal grinned ruefully. He had learned that Longbraids knew what he was talking about.

"You weren't trying to twist his tail at the same time?" Cal asked quizzically.

This was the first time Cal had heard Longbraids laugh. It was a soft, happy sound. "Maybe," Longbraids confessed. "But I would not like to see anything bad happen to the D bar S. I work for it, too."

That was all the loyalty Cal could ask for. "You've been in those prairie fires, Joe?"

"Twice." Longbraids' eyes darkened at the memory. "I lost cattle in the last one."

"Is there any way to fight them?"

Longbraids shrugged before answering. "You can use hope and a lot of prayers. That's not the most effective way. There's only two ways I know of to fight a fire. You can kill a big steer and drag him across the line of fire, smothering the blaze."

Cal frowned. He didn't care too much for that method. It meant the loss of an animal.

Longbraids must have guessed what Cal's frown meant, for he nodded in sympathy. "I like the fire drags better."

This was something new to Cal. "What's that, Joe?"

"They're made of chains and twelve-foot asbestos sheets," Longbraids answered. "The whole thing drags on heavy steel links. One of them will wear out the six saddle horses dragging it.

From just this meager description, Cal could see

how effective those drags could be, fighting a fire. "Do you know where you can get a couple of them?" he asked.

"Maybe," Longbraids answered. "I might be able to buy them from the Indian families. It would take time to locate them. And money," he added.

"Find them," Cal said promptly, "and buy them." Now he could understand Longbraids' hesitancy. Pardee would scream at what seemed to him an unnecessary preparation. Right now, the country was green and lush. It was ridiculous to be worrying about a fire now. "Pardee doesn't have to know a thing about it," Cal said.

This was another first—Cal saw Longbraids smile, an unreserved display of feeling. A strong bond was building between the two of them, a bond formed of understanding and respect.

"I'll find them," Longbraids said.

"Good," Cal replied gruffly. "We'd better be heading back before Pardee sends out a search party for us."

Even though the cattle chores were down to a minimum, the work never lessened. There were corrals to be built, and permanent fords to be constructed over the deeper streams. The deep green lushness of the foliage dulled as spring faded into summer and the sun grew fiercer. Cal thought many times of his talk with Longbraids about the fire drags. Longbraids had found two of them, had them brought up and hidden in a thicket. Cal hoped there would never be any use for them, but just the same, he felt better about having them. So far, Pardee hadn't seen the drags. A couple of times, Cal was sure Pardee would ride onto them, but at the last instant, something happened to change his course. Each time, Cal blew out a weak breath of relief. He could just imagine how Pardee would roar, "What're these damnfool contraptions?" How the volume of the roar would increase when he learned what Cal had paid for them.

Cal was almost content with this life, except for the times he thought wistfully of Hale not being with them. Morning after morning, Cal had awakened thinking, Hale will ride in today. Even as he thought that, he knew the hope was futile. Hale had inherited that stiff-necked pride from Pardee. Often Cal had wondered what Hale was doing now. He hoped everything was turning out well for him. Cal also thought often of Ellie. Each time that hollow in his stomach came back, and each time he admonished himself with the thought, you can't have everything your way. This was the life he had chosen, and he had never heard of any life that didn't have a few flaws.

He rode with Pardee, enjoying the appearance of every bunch of cattle they passed. The improvement in those cattle was striking. Those sharp edges of backbones had disappeared, and fat was beginning to lard those once stark ribs.

"They've put on pounds and pounds, Pa." Cal couldn't keep the exultation out of his voice. "We can ship this fall." God, he hoped so. It had been far too long since the Deckers had seen any marketable cattle.

The prospects should have lightened Pardee's face, but it remained stonily impassive. Dammit, Cal thought. What did it take to put some enthusiasm into his father.

"We'd better," Pardee said grimly. "We're running out of money. We were almost broke when we left Texas, and I sure haven't seen any money coming in."

Cal looked at him in surprise. What brought on that outburst?

"Ever since I was a kid, the old timers told me this was the rottenest business a man could get into." Pardee was wound up and couldn't stop. "If the weather didn't hurt you, the varmints would. After those two, there was always a bad market waiting to grab what was left. They told me I'd handle a lot of money, but not one of those dollars would ever really belong to me. Somebody would have their hands out, trying to snatch that dollar away. The only time a cattleman ever had any money that he might be able to stick into his pocket was when he sold out everything he owned, the land, the cattle, and the horses. Looks like they knew what they were talking about, don't it?" he finished gloomily.

Cal got a glimpse of all the strain filled years Pardee had known. No wonder he was irascible so much of the time. Maybe Pardee had every right to feel sorry for himself, but Cal couldn't allow that.

"We're still alive, Pa, and we've got a brand new chance. We'll pull out. Next year will be even better."

"Next year, next year," Pardee snarled. "I'm sick of those two words." He got a hold on his temper and smoothed out his face. "Hell, Cal." That could be sheepishness in his tone. "I know that. Every year I know the next one will be better. What do you think keeps me going on?"

They rode a long way, and Cal hated to bring up this subject, for it was another blow at Pardee's already drained finances.

"Pa, we're about out of supplies. I thought I'd

take a wagon into town tomorrow and load up what we need."

Pardee frowned at him. "That's usually Deke's job."

"He buys like he has to pay for everything out of his own pocket," Cal said heatedly. "Always the poorest and cheapest food he can find." At the storm gathering in Pardee's face, Cal rushed on to bolster his argument. "How many mornings straight have we had oatmeal?" Lumpy oatmeal at that, Cal could have added.

That shook Pardee a little. "Anybody bellyaching about the food except you?" Pardee's fierce eyes stabbed into Cal.

He's still protecting Briscoe, Cal thought wearily. "Everybody," Cal said flatly. "I've heard some of the men say about all a man gets out of life is what he puts in his belly. Their bellies haven't had much to be happy about for a good while now." He didn't name those unhappy bellies; he didn't want Pardee jumping all over them.

That jolted Pardee. His face was stiff and he gave what Cal said long thought, then conceded. "All right. You buy the supplies. We'll see how much better you can do."

Cal felt Pardee was being unfair, but he kept silent. The food he bought would still have to be cooked by Briscoe. Briscoe could ruin any kind of food. All right, Cal thought in resignation. He was ready to take the blame, since going into town would give him a chance to see Hale. Another reason for going kept creeping into his mind. He wanted to see Ellie, too.

Chapter Eleven

CAL TIED THE team and wagon to the hitchrack before the hotel. He walked in, his heart beating like a drum. Until now, he hadn't realized how badly he wanted to see Ellie.

He masked the disappointment that flooded over him. Ellie was at the desk all right, but Hobart was with her. Maybe Cal could find some way to get rid of him so that he could talk to Ellie alone.

Both of their heads were bent over some work before them, and they didn't see nor hear Cal until he spoke.

"Hello there," Cal said. He groaned at the inaneness of the remark. Why couldn't he come up with something brilliant? His memory had tricked him; Ellie was far prettier than he had remembered.

Ellie looked up at Cal's words, but there was no greeting in her eyes. Cal thought in dismay, if he read those frozen eyes right, he was the last person Ellie wanted to see.

"I came into town to see Hale," Cal said lamely. "Is he in?"

"Did you come to jump all over him again?" Ellie asked tartly.

Cal stared at her astounded. What was she talking about?

"He told me all about it," she said coldly. "How his father never wanted to see him again."

Cal met the ferocity of her eyes and stared her down. So Hale had told her all about the split between him and his father. Hale had a tendency to run off at the mouth. Cal softened the harshness of that judgment. If he had been in Hale's place and with a pretty ear to pour his troubles into, Cal knew he would have done the same thing.

He shook his head. "That was between Pardee and Hale. I had no part of it."

Maybe her eyes softened some, but her words were still accusatory. "Maybe so. But you're still with your father, aren't you?"

That outraged Cal. Wasn't the rift in the Decker family bad enough? Did she expect him to walk out on Pardee, too. With sickening clarity, Cal knew Ellie was behind Hale one hundred percent. Hale had used his time with her well.

Ellie's belligerence was still evident, and Cal said gently, "He's my brother. I only wanted to see him."

Hobart had been watching the tension that was building between Ellie and Cal with worried eyes. Cal's words must have reassured him, for he let out a sigh.

"He isn't in right now," he said. "He's not in very often. I don't know when that boy finds time to sleep."

Dammit, Cal thought. Hale was still at the poker table. It wasn't possible that his streak of good luck had lasted this long, but it seemed so.

"Hale still winning?" Cal asked casually.

Hobart shook his head. "Hale hasn't got time to play much poker any more. His hands are too full with other things."

Hobart glanced at his daughter, and she nodded her permission for him to go on. Cal noticed something about her for the first time. She was absolutely radiant. All the tenseness Cal had seen in her before was gone. She looked as though all burdens had been lifted from her shoulders.

"What's he doing?" Cal asked curiously.

"Buying up the town," Hobart answered promptly. "He's got his hands into everything. I tell you that boy is a genius. He's brought new life to this town. I don't know what we would have done without his help. You tell him, Ellie."

Cal had never seen such a sweet smile, and Ellie's eyes were soft with a memory.

"We were in bad trouble," Ellie said. "No, that's being mild. We were broke, and there was no place to turn. Hale pried it out of me, and he insisted upon putting money into the hotel. Sam and I wouldn't take it until Hale accepted thirty percent of the hotel. I told Hale he had to consider it an investment. He finally agreed. It was the oddest thing. Right after he helped us, things turned around. The hotel started making money. Hale is getting a return on his investment."

Cal was glad to hear that, for all of them, but Ellie was giving Hale undue credit. Hale just happened to step in at the right time. With the lease land filling up, new people were bound to be drawn to Evarts. When those people came to Evarts, they had to have someplace to stay. Hale's timing was just one of those lucky things. Wisely, Cal didn't try to point that out of her. Ellie would have snapped his head off. No, it was all Hale's doing and nobody could low talk him to Ellie.

She's lost to me, Cal realized as he looked at her. Damn that lucky Hale. Everything worked out in his favor. Cal wanted to cuss at the inequities of life. Some people were just born blessed, and Hale was one of those.

"Isn't that fine," Cal said heartily. There was no false note in his voice. "You still haven't told me where I can find him."

"He's opened up an office a block down the street," Ellie said. "He calls it the Land Development Company. You can't miss it."

Cal was well aware of the radiance in Ellie's face, and her voice was vibrant as she spoke about Hale. Cal's sense of loss increased. Perhaps there was no definite understanding between Hale and this girl, but Ellie Hobart was obviously in love with Hale. Cal could see it as though it was written in letters six feet tall.

He started for the door, and Ellie asked, "We'll see you again?"

She sounded sincere, but it wasn't because of him, Cal thought. It was only because he was Hale's brother.

"Sure," he answered steadily.

As he reached the door, a voice hailed him, and he turned to see Doctor Mathews coming down the stairs. Mathews joined him and asked, "Have any more trouble with that hand?"

"After a couple of days, I never thought any more about it," Cal answered. Mathews had a retentive memory.

Mathews beamed. "Hale never had any more trouble, either. I'll call on you two when I need a testimonial for a new patient."

"You do that," Cal said and smiled.

"Seen Hale lately?" Mathews asked.

"On my way there now," Cal replied. He hoped Mathews hadn't heard about the rift between Hale and Pardee. Cal didn't want to talk about it.

"Good," Mathews replied. "I'm going that way. Your brother is cutting a wide swath, isn't he?"

"So I've heard," Cal answered.

Mathews peered at him, and Cal wondered if Mathews had detected a note of jealousy in his voice. Cal didn't want that. He was glad for everything good that had happened to Hale.

"Maybe he wasn't meant to chase cows around, Doc," Cal said steadily.

Mathews nodded. "That could be. My God, the way he rushes around. Makes some of us old timers see what can be done." He cackled in sudden amusement. "The only excuse I can see for myself is that Hale's young." He paused in reflection. "But I didn't do anything like's he's doing when I was young. It makes me tired just thinking about him. He's one of the rare ones, the kind that doesn't come along often."

Cal was beginning to get a little weary of hearing everybody sing Hale's praise. Dammit, he knew Hale from a long way back. He could tell some tales that would shock all these admirers. He grinned faintly at a few memories. Of course, he wasn't going to open his mouth about those tales. But the Hale he knew and the one he was hearing about sounded like two different people. Something had really twisted Hale's tail.

"What did you say, Doc?" Cal hadn't been listening, and apologized.

"You were off somewhere," Mathews agreed.

He pointed at a restaurant across the street. "I'm going in there for a late breakfast. Care to join me?"

Cal shook his head. "Already eaten, Doc."

"When you're in town again and need a good meal, there's the place. I used to dread mealtime because the food was so poor in this town. I'd reach for a bottle instead of making the effort to go out." His eyes widened with a sudden thought. "Hell, that restaurant might cure my drinking. Naw," he said grinning at Hall. "All it can do is to slow it down a little."

Cal had a sudden suspicion. "Don't tell me Hale's behind that restaurant?"

"He sure is." Mathews beamed. "Hale used to scream his head off about there not being a decent place to eat in town. He didn't just talk; he went out and did something about it." Mathews sensed the question in Cal's mind. "No, Hale isn't running it. He found the best cook in town and bankrolled her. She's about run all the other restaurants out of town. She can't help but be making money."

Cal thought of the saloon, the hotel, and now this. "My God," he said. "Is there anything in town that he hasn't got his thumb into?"

Mathews chuckled. "If there is, Hale hasn't heard about it. Sure you won't join me?"

"Some other time," Cal replied. As he watched Mathews cross the street, he began to examine his feelings honestly. Damn, he was proud of that kid brother of his. He was only envious of Hale's success because of the standing it had given him with Ellie.

Cal found Hale's office with no difficulty. He stood at the window for a long moment. Everything about the office was spotlessly clean and new. It had a unique smell about it, and Cal had to analyze that smell before he could come up with an answer. It was the smell of money.

Hale's head was bent over some work on his desk, and he didn't see Cal staring at him. He looks damned good, Cal thought. So far, city life hadn't softened Hale in the slightest. If anything, he looked leaner, more sharp. He's plumb grown up, Cal thought before he moved to the door.

Cal stepped inside and drawled, "Mister, could you stake a down and outer to a meal."

Hale lifted his head, stared incredulously at Cal, then whopped with joy. He sprang to his feet, bounded around the desk, and fell on Cal, mauling him happily.

He hasn't lost any muscle tone yet, Cal thought as he backed away to save himself from further punishment.

"Are you trying to beat me to death?" he complained.

Hale stopped his pummelling, but the grin never left his face. "I never thought I'd see the time when I'd be glad to see you." He surveyed Cal critically, then said, "You don't look like you've missed too many meals.

"I'm getting by," Cal answered. Hale's eyes were filled with a big question, and Cal waited for Hale to ask it.

Hale hemmed and hawed, then finally blurted out, "How's Pa?"

"Good," Cal said. "Renting this lease was the smartest thing he ever did. Pa looks better with every pound the cattle put on."

"I'm glad to hear that," Hale said. He walked

to his desk and sat down, waving Cal to a chair opposite him. He reached in a drawer and pulled out a bottle and two glasses. He poured them full and shoved one toward Cal.

He grinned at Cal's hesitation. "You don't have to worry about this whiskey. This is the bottle I keep for special people."

"I wasn't thinking of that," Cal said. "I was only thinking, it's a little early."

"Not when we haven't seen each other for so long," Hale said decisively.

Cal couldn't argue with that. He downed his drink. This was good whiskey. It slid down smoothly and prodded gently around in a man's stomach, instead of hauling off and kicking him with a mule's hoof. From what Cal had heard, Hale could well afford this kind of whiskey. He noticed that Hale only sipped at his drink. Cal remembered times when Hale used to punish this stuff.

Cal spoke the question that was paramount in both their minds. "When are you going to ride over and see Pa?"

He saw the familiar jutting of Hale's jaw and sighed. That old stubbornness was showing again.

"Never," Hale said harshly. "You heard him. He said I was no longer his son. A lot of people heard him."

Cal saw it was useless to argue with him. Two stiff-necked people had clashed in a match of wills, and neither was yet ready to make the first move at mending the break. Maybe the timing for it was all wrong; all Cal could do was to hope that one of these days it would come.

To change the painful subject Cal said, "Been hearing a lot of things about you, boy."

Hale's grin showed his embarrassment. "A lot of luck, Cal. I got my hands on a sizable amount of money, and it seemed there were better things to do with it than just putting it back into a poker game. You've been talking to Ellie," he accused.

"And to Doc Mathews. They think you are some kind of wonder."

"Aw," Hale made a deprecatory gesture. "Things just broke right."

"Tell me about it," Cal invited. At Hale's hesitation, he said, "I won't think you're bragging."

Hale drew a deep breath. He wanted to talk about his good luck; it was written all over his face. "I bought a few town lots, Cal. The railroad wants some of them to build new offices on. The railroad believes this country will grow, too. I just happened to have the lots they wanted." He threw back his head and laughed joyously. "I closed the deal with them a couple of days ago, and stuck them good. I figured they owed me for that miserable train ride."

Cal couldn't help but grin. "Good for you."

Hale leaned forward, his face earnest. "This country is bound to grow, Hale. It has to with all the new cattle money flowing into it. I just happened to be in the right place at the right time. My poker playing that outraged Pa so gave me a little money to play with." He held up three fingers. "I learned a man can't miss if he has these three things with him." He ticked off the fingers one at a time. "Money, the right time, the right place."

Cal couldn't argue with that. But how in the hell did a man put them all together. Maybe Hale should have ticked off the fourth finger, lots of luck.

"You're smarter than Pardee and me," Cal said. "We didn't see the possibilities."

"You never had time to see anything but raising cattle," Hale said thoughtfully. He added hastily, "But that's what you wanted. I got shoved into something else." He stared bleakly at the opposite wall, and Cal knew he was thinking of Pardee again.

"I'm going back into cattle again, Cal," Hale went on. "In a kinda different way. I'm thinking of buying into the ferry, or maybe buying it outright, if old man Struthers decides to retire. The last time I talked to him he told me he's made too many trips across the river."

Cal couldn't help that little stab of envy. Hale could fall into a dark hole and come up with his hands full of gold. Cal thought of all the cattle the ferry had already carried and of the more to come. Then the shipment back across the river would start, taking those cattle to market when they were ready.

"It'll be a moneymaker, Hale," he said. The envy was all gone and again Cal was just damned proud of his brother.

The talk went to shared experiences they'd had while growing up.

"Remember how you whipped my butt every time you thought I got out of line, Cal?" Hale chuckled. "I always swore I would even that up. It never happened, did it?"

"No," Cal agreed gently. Those scores would never be evened up now. They were both grown men, and another violent clash between them would probably never come.

"What do you think of Ellie?" Hale asked abruptly.

"She belongs with that special bottle of yours."

Hale looked pleased. "I think so, too. I'm going to marry that girl one of these days."

Cal knew this was coming; still he felt as though he had lost his stomach, leaving only that familiar hollow. Hale was wrong when he said he never whipped Cal. He had whipped Cal thoroughly in this last struggle, the most important one.

Cal managed to keep his voice true. "You asked her yet?"

"No. I'm just waiting for the right time."

Cal stared steadily at him. Hale wasn't as bright as he thought he was, or he was overly cautious. The time was already here. Anybody with an ounce of sense in his head could see that.

Cal stood and said, "I've got to buy some supplies. I better be getting at it." He stuck out his hand. "Be seeing you again soon."

"You'd better," Hale threatened. "Or I'll try once more to whip your ass, if you don't."

Cal wanted to ask once more if Hale would bend his stiff neck and make an effort to see Pardee. He remembered that hard line of Hale's jaw when it was first mentioned, and let go of the impulse. Nothing he could say would change Hale's mind.

Hale walked to the door with Cal, his arm around his brother's shoulders. "The next time you come in you promise you'll look me up."

"I promise," Cal said solemnly.

He didn't look back as he walked to the team and untied it from the rack. If only there was some way he could tell Pardee about Hale's success. He knew it was useless. He wouldn't get a half-dozen words out before Pardee would roar, "Shut your damned mouth." Cal was proud of Hale. Pardee would be, too, if he would only listen. "Two damned hardheads," he muttered as he climbed up onto the seat.

Chapter Twelve

UNDER THE STEADILY strengthening summer sun, the grass dried, turning the range into a sea of yellow as far as the eye could see. The cattle seemed to like the dried grass as well as they had before, and Cal could see no loss in their weight. Those four-year old steers were getting absolutely fat. The D bar S was going to make its fall shipment.

Cal never said anything more to Longbraids about the fire drags, though he thought about them constantly. Even if this wasn't the fire season, it seemed closer to it than Cal cared to be.

He rode with his eye cocked on the sky. Lord, it had been weeks since it had rained, and Cal prayed for moisture to take the dry crackling out of the grass. But thunder and lightning usually came with rain. Cal wouldn't mind so much if the lightning came while it was raining; the rain would wet down the potential fire danger. But if a bolt hit this dried grass before it rained, it would touch the grass off like a match.

Everybody Cal talked to spoke of nothing but the possibilities of fire. So far, no one had reported any fire, but that didn't lessen the anxiety.

Cal sat out in front of the house after supper, watching the dark mass of clouds building up in the west. Was it possible that a good rain was coming?

He looked up as Longbraids sat down beside him. "Enjoy your meal, Joe?"

Longbraids' grunt was more eloquent than a long tirade.

Cal grinned. "You don't have to say it. That meal was pretty bad. Briscoe gets worse all the time. I keep comparing them with the meals you cooked while we were looking over the lease."

Longbraids shook his head and didn't answer.

Cal knew that while Longbraids hadn't said a work about the Briscoes, he didn't like them. He had caught too many veiled, weighing glances Longbraids gave the Briscoes. Dent and Jude Briscoe had tried to make life miserable for Longbraids, until Cal had stepped in and stopped them.

"You let me see you two deviling him in any way, and you're out on your butts," he warned them. "If you think that's just talk, try me."

Since then Cal had kept the Briscoes off of Longbraids, but he was always watchful. He never knew what might pop into those two heads, particularly if they were liquored up. Pardee had a strict order against drinking on the job, but Cal knew the Briscoes brought whiskey back every time they went into town. Still, he hadn't been able to catch them at it.

"Looks like we're going to get a rain, Joe."

Longbraids studied the clouds, then shook his head. "Not much," he disagreed. "Very little rain in those clouds. Plenty of wind and lightning though."

Cal didn't try to argue with him. He had learned Longbraids was right about most things that happened in nature.

Before Cal could speak a vivid streak of lightning slashed through the skies, illuminating the masses of clouds, and the deep rumble of faraway thunder sounded.

That bolt had to strike somewhere, and Cal prayed it wasn't on the D bar S land.

It had opened up the skies to the damnest electrical storm Cal had ever witnessed. Long, jagged streaks of lightning crisscrossed the sky in every direction. Cal groaned. This was what he had been fearing; plenty of lightning with no rain.

"Maybe it isn't hitting on us," he said hopefully.

Longbraids grunted and stood abruptly. "I've got a lot to do." He stalked off before Cal could reply.

Cal stared after him. What could be driving Longbraids now? It was dark, and surely Longbraids could put off what he thought he had to do until morning.

Cal sat there a long time, watching the electrical display, wincing every time those clouds were scissored by another bolt. He stood and shook himself impatiently. Sitting out here wasn't doing him a bit of good. He might as well get some sleep. He lay awake a long time, hoping to hear the patter of rain on the roof.

Cal was the first one up in the morning. He walked outside and cursed. Not a damned drop of rain had fallen, and the sky was clear. The sun was just beginning to rise; it was going to be another hot, dry day.

Longbraids came up to him, and Cal said wryly, "Looks like you were right again."

Longbraids looked as though he hadn't gotten a wink of sleep. Cal started to ask why, but Longbraids waved his words away.

"Look," he said, pointing to the west.

Cal followed the pointing finger, and a lump of fear lodged in his throat. There was no mistaking what that wavering gray plume was; smoke from a fire set off by last night's electrical storm.

"How far away?" Cal asked.

"Pretty far right now," Longbraids replied. "Come." He started to move away, and Cal checked him.

"I'll be with you in a minute," he said. "I've got to tell Pardee about this."

Longbraids nodded. Understanding was in the gesture but so was impatience.

Cal hurried inside and shook Pardee awake. Pardee glared at him for disturbing the last few sweet moments of sleep.

"Fire," Cal said. "To the west. I don't know how bad it is, but those four-year olds better be moved."

That wiped the last vestige of sleep from Pardee's eyes, leaving a sick dismay.

"How bad is it?" he asked as he reached for his pants.

"Don't know yet," Cal replied tersely. "Longbraids and I are on the way to see. Pa, get the others on their feet. Bring all the horses." Cal didn't know how many horses would be needed, but he wanted to be on the safe side. "Tell Briscoe to hitch up the chuck wagon." They might well need the water barrels on each side of the wagon, and if fighting the fire turned into a long battle, the men would have to be fed.

Pardee sat down and pulled on his boots. His face was gray, and Cal knew this new worry was the cause. He wouldn't be surprised if Pardee cussed his head off, but his father rarely used words where they would do him no good.

"I'll see you out there," Cal said and ran outside.

Longbraids hadn't wasted any time. He had Cal's horse saddled and was waiting to hand Cal the reins.

Cal didn't ask any questions. He would find out soon enough where Longbraids was going. He nodded as Longbraids headed for the thicket where the fire drags were hidden. Cal prayed they wouldn't have to use the drags, but if they did, Pardee would owe Longbraids a huge thanks for having them ready.

Twenty mounted Indians waited for them at the thicket. At Cal's surprise, Longbraids explained, "I went around last night, asking them to come. They've fought fire before. I told them the D bar S would pay them."

"Hell, yes," Cal said. This was the answer to why Longbraids looked weary. Instead of sleeping, he had spent the night finding help. Maybe Pardee wouldn't admit it, but hiring Longbraids was one of the smartest things Cal ever did.

The Indians tied their ropes to the steel rings, welded onto the heavy bars along one end of the drags. It would take six horses to move each of those cumbersome things. The Indians mounted and secured the other end of their ropes around the saddle horns.

One of them lifted his hand to Longbraids, and Cal and Longbraids moved out at a slow trot.

Cal looked frequently over his shoulders. Those drags were putting a tremendous load on the horses. Under this kind of pressure, a horse would wear out quickly. The D bar S would need every horse they had before this day was through.

Every time Cal looked at that plume of smoke, it seemed to grow in volume. A coyote bitch and her six half grown cubs streaked past Cal. Ordinarily, Cal would have made every effort to eradicate the predators, but now, his mind was too occupied to do more than barely notice them.

The closer he got to the fire, the more small animals he saw, scurrying through the grass, intent on escaping the fire and smoke. Over to his left, Cal saw the first bunch of the four-year old steers. A few had stopped grazing, their heads lifted, as they uneasily sniffed the heat-laden air. The others went on with their grazing. Cattle weren't as survival-wise as wild animals when it came to something like this.

It looked as though the whole world was on fire. It had started on Circle A land, across the fence, but pushed by a strong breeze, it was steadily creeping their way. The fire was already on D bar S land. The only thing Cal could see to their advantage was that a relatively narrow neck of D bar S land touched the Circle A. If the fire could be held in this neck, it might be whipped. Once it was beyond the neck it would spread out rapidly.

These Indians knew what they were doing. They didn't need a word or signal from Longbraids to put the drags into motion, pulling them at right angles to the line of fire. They kicked their horses into faster motion, and now the real pressure started on the mounts.

The Indians pulled the drags in tandem, chewing up the grass in a twenty-four foot swath. The steel circles on the bottom of the drags, broke the grass into small bits and plowed it under.

Cal looked back at the ever lengthening swath. Was the breeze strong enough to make the fire jump that swath? Only time could tell.

Cal, Longbraids, and the other dismounted Indians followed on foot, alert for the smallest spark. Cal saw his first one, a tiny blackening circle, the fire strengthening at its edge. He stomped it furiously, not stopping until he was sure the small fire was dead.

Cal looked around him, and Longbraids and the other Indians were extinguishing other sparks. Even if the fire burned up to the edge of the swath and died, those damned sparks could be their undoing.

Cal stomped like a man gone berserk, trying to eliminate the little spreading circles that threatened to undo all of their efforts. In a half-hour, his legs were limber weak, and he gasped for breath. He found out that this was the hardest work a man could do. He stopped a moment to try to shake the dizziness out of his head and to clear his eyes. The exhaustion creeping into him was the culmination of savage effort, and anxiety.

Cal forced himself on, his eyes to the ground, trying to spot the next insidious enemy. Where in the hell was Pardee? Cal needed fresh horses. The ones on the drags were showing extreme distress. Their heads were low, and they foamed at the muzzle. Their excessive sweating turned their coats several degrees darker. They must have fresh horses soon, and he needed more help.

Cal turned his head at the hard pound of hoofs and blew out a breath of relief. Pardee and the others were coming, and the chuck wagon was right behind them.

Pardee sprang to the ground beside Cal. The worry was riding him hard; the grayness in his face had increased.

"We got the steers moved." Pardee gestured at a handful of steers a few hundred yards away. "Missed them. Too big a hurry to waste more time on them. I left four of the boys to keep them from wandering back. I brought the rest with me." He asked the question uppermost in his mind. "How's it going?"

Cal looked back along the swath. They had covered a little more than half of the distance to the far side of the neck. They were winning, but they hadn't won; up ahead, that remorseless line of fire crept ever closer.

"Pa, if we can confine the fire in this neck, we've got it whipped. We need more horses on those drags."

Pardee's eyes bulged as he stared at the strange contrivances. "What the hell are those damned contraptions?"

Cal grinned wanly. Pardee used almost exactly the words Cal thought he would use when he first saw the drags.

"Fire drags," Cal said. "Built for just this purpose. Longbraids knew all about them and told me. You can thank him for finding those two. We had them hidden in a thicket for just such an emergency." His grin strengthened. "I didn't want you raising hell until you saw their usefulness."

Pardee pursed his lips and stared speculatively at Longbraids, then Cal. Cal could relax. Pardee wasn't going to say anything. All the ground had been cut from under his feet.

"The horses on those drags are just about worn out," Cal suggested.

"I got eyes, ain't I?" Pardee demanded testily. He whirled and yelled at the wranglers bringing up the remuda. "Get a dozen fresh horses up here," he bellowed. "Move, dammit!"

A thought occurred to Cal as he watched fresh horses replacing the tired ones. Hale had said a man couldn't lose when he was in the right place at the right time. Both of those factors were in Cal's favor here. Maybe now, he could think ahead to winning.

He waited impatiently for the chuck wagon to reach them. Maybe Briscoe was lashing all the speed he could get from the team of mules, but to a waiting man, it seemed as though they merely crawled.

"You took your time," Cal said acidly as the wagon ground to a stop.

A flush mottled Briscoe's face as he yelled in outrage. "I took time to fill up the water barrels. I can't do anything to suit you."

"All right, all right," Cal said coldly. This time, he was dead wrong, but he wasn't going to admit it and he was relieved Pardee wasn't close enough to hear that exchange.

"Joe," Cal called and beckoned Longbraids over. "Bring the others." If they wanted a drink as badly as he did, they were hurting.

Cal drank until his thirst was satisfied, then poured a cup of water over his head. A while back he would have doubted it, but he was going to live.

He waited until the others slaked their thirst, then said to Longbraids, "Joe, get the blankets out of the wagon and douse them in the barrels."

Longbraids nodded his understanding. He knew what Cal wanted. A soaked blanket was a far more effective tool in extinguishing a spark than a man's boot heel. The men whose blankets would be used in this manner, would squawk their heads off when they heard about it. Cal shook his head at the thought. This fire was costing Pardee quite a bit of money. He erased that thought by thinking it would cost Pardee a lot more, if the fire got away and ravaged acres of D bar S land.

A thin line of men followed the two drags, flailing away at every spark with wet blankets. The fresh horses put more speed into the drags, and it taxed Cal's legs to even keep up with them. Now, he was getting complaints from his legs and arms. All limbs were beginning to ache like bad teeth. Cal swung his blanket until he thought his arms would drop out of their sockets. The exhaustion was creeping up on him again, and his breathing was a harsh, tearing sound. That light-headed dizziness was reaching for him again.

Longbraids worked a few feet from Cal. He looked at Cal and saw something that made him drop his blanket. He rushed over to Cal and beat with open hands against the small of Cal's back.

"You gone crazy," Cal squawked and tried to escape from the mauling.

Longbraids almost grinned again. "A spark landed on your back. It was spreading."

Cal felt the small of his back and his fingers explored a hole in his shirt as big as his doubled fists. He didn't actually feel pain, but the small of his back was sensitive.

"Thanks, Joe," He said. "I owe you. I didn't even feel it." He was either too absorbed in his fire fighting or the spark had landed in a loose fold of his shirt. It couldn't have spread much farther before Cal would have felt the heat.

Longbraids was sober faced, but his eyes were dancing. "You prove what I've always thought."

"What?" Cal asked suspiciously.

"I always thought the white man had little feeling."

Cal chuckled in spite of his efforts to keep his face straight. "Forget I said I owed you one. You just evened the score." He felt as comfortable with this man as any man he had ever known. He hoped Longbraids felt the same, though he doubted he would ever get such an admission out of him.

"I think we're going to make it, Joe," Cal said.

Longbraids looked dubiously at the remaining distance. "It's going to be close. Maybe you'd better put fresh horses on the drags."

Cal nodded. That would be his appraisal of the situation. The fire was creeping ever closer to the line of the swath. He looked back along the swath, and the fire had died out against it. From now on it would be touch and go.

Cal turned and yelled at a wrangler. "Pete. New horses." He held up the ten fingers of his two hands, then added two more.

He wanted to sit down while the saddles were changed, but he didn't dare. He knew if he did, he wouldn't be able to get up.

Longbraids looked at the drags before the horses started again and shook his head. Cal joined him and saw the reason for the concern in Longbraids' face. The drags were almost worn out. They had turned into a tangled mess of twisted chains and steel, and the asbestos sheets were beaten into a pulp.

"They won't go much farther," Longbraids said.

Cal wanted to scream. They had come this close to winning, then to fail by so little, made him sick in his guts.

"We're not done yet," Longbraids said. "If Pardee doesn't stop us, we could shoot a couple of steers and use their carcasses to replace the drags."

Cal's eyes widened. The carcasses wouldn't be as effective as the drags, but at this stage he was willing to try anything.

He looked around, and Pardee wasn't in sight. "Let's go shoot them," he said. He felt he didn't have time to look up Pardee, nor to try and explain anything to him. Even the suggestion of such an action would drive Pardee wild.

Cal and Longbraids rode out and shot the two biggest steers they could find. Cal looked at the sightless eyes and knew how Pardee felt. This was horror to a cattleman seeing his animals destroyed like this.

He threw a loop around a steer's hind legs, and Longbraids roped the other. They dragged the two bodies to the fire drags, and they were none too soon, for the drags were done. Only a few shreds of asbestos remained among the tangled chains.

Cal and Longbraids took over one steer, each with a rope around the front and hind legs. They fanned out a little and spurred their mounts into action. Looking behind him, Cal saw two Indians doing the same with the other carcass.

This wasn't nearly as effective as the drags, for the bouncing bodies didn't rip and tear out the grass as the chain links had done. But the weight of the carcasses was breaking and beating the grass down into the ground, lessening the fuel for the ravenous fire.

Men on foot followed the two steers, flailing frantically at every little tongue of fire that showed. They had far more work to do than when the drags were used, and they fought with frenzied activity. Cal looked behind him frequently but could see no spots where the fire was spreading on this side of the swath.

He and Longbraids finished up on top of the steep bank that dropped sharply to the creek. It was almost a tie, for the first licking tongues of fire arrived shortly after Cal and Longbraids did.

Cal and Longbraids stomped like two crazy men. God, they ached for one of those wet blankets, but there wasn't time to go after them.

They beat out the last of the flames, and Cal braced his legs to keep from falling on his face. Some grass ran down the steep bank, but it was sparse, and Cal didn't think it was enough to feed the fire's appetite and keep it alive. Besides, the width of the creek should stop the flames from jumping the water. Cal wanted to yell they had the fire licked, but he didn't dare jinx the moment by saying it. There would be time for exaltation after every spark, every ember was dead.

"We'd better get back and see if they need help," Cal said.

Longbraids grimaced, but he nodded. The grimace was the only admission he would make that he was just as tired as Cal.

Cal found a dozen men standing around the chuck wagon. The hadn't reached the end of the swath, and Cal was sure more sparks would fly over it. He tore angrily into them and Granger said, "Whoa. Back up. Look at this." He held up his tattered blanket. It was so hot it was smoking in spots. "We came up to resoak the blankets and get a drink. The water barrels are empty."

"Where's Briscoe?" Cal demanded. He was so angry he shook.

"Look under the wagon," Granger said.

Cal bent down and looked. Briscoe was sound asleep. Cal reached under the wagon, seized an arm, and dragged Briscoe out.

Briscoe awakened hard. He stared stupidly about him, and spluttered, "What the hell?"

Cal wanted to kick him. "The water barrels are empty." He was determined not to lose his temper, but it rose steadily and his voice got away from him. He wound up by screaming, "Everybody needs water, and the blankets are dry." His words tumbled out so fast they ran together. "By God, you worthless bastard. If we lose this fire, I'll hang you with my own hands."

That frightened Briscoe, and his eyes rolled. He gulped and said in a weak voice, "Dammit, Cal. I've worked my tail off. I just crawled under there to catch some rest. I can't go any farther."

Briscoe looked uneasily about him. Maybe he hoped to see Pardee or maybe he was afraid that he would. Cal didn't know which.

"You get those barrels filled and get back within a half-hour. Or don't bother to come back."

Briscoe stared sullenly at the ground. "Jesus, Cal, I can't do that all by myself."

"Then you'd better find Jude and Dent," Cal said grimly. "I haven't seen them do much today." He looked around at the grinning faces. The men enjoyed hearing and seeing Briscoe taken apart, but the faces smoothed out under Cal's savage eyes.

"Who's got a watch?" Cal demanded.

Granger pulled out one and held it up for Cal to see.

"Eight o'clock, Briscoe," he snapped. "If you want to stay on the payroll, you better be back here by eight-thirty."

Briscoe's eyes were murderous, but he didn't dare open his mouth. He scrambled into the wagon and savagely lashed the mules.

Granger stood beside Cal, watching the dust clouds Briscoe raised. "Never saw him move so fast." Something else was on his mind, and he dared to put it into words. "Cal, why does Pardee keep Briscoe on?"

"That's Pardee's business," Cal said. He wasn't about to talk about Pardee's shortcomings with anybody.

Cal asked Granger what time it was four different times during the next half-hour. The last time he asked, Granger replied, "Eight-twenty seven." There was undisguised disgust in his voice. "Oh, dammit. He made it. Here he comes now." He grinned wolfishly at Cal. "I was hoping to see you hang him."

Cal watched Briscoe pull the wagon up beside him. Jude and Dent sat on the seat with their father. All three faces were sullen, and Cal hoped any one of them would open his mouth.

"All right," he said roughly. "You made it. Now, I want a hot supper for the men. Have it ready when we get through."

He locked eyes with Briscoe, hoping Briscoe would make some complaint about that order. But Briscoe's eyes couldn't hold steady, and they slid away.

The blankets were resoaked, and everybody slaked their thirst before they went back to work. Darkness fell, and they still hunted the last little spreading circle of fire. The darkness helped in one way; it enabled them to see the little licking tongues of flame.

Longbraids, working beside Cal, stopped and lifted his head. "The wind's changing, Cal. I think you can safely say you've beaten it now."

It wasn't a single man's victory, Cal thought; all of them shared in this one. Even the Briscoes had a small part.

Everybody covered the length of the swath once more, on foot. None of them found a single dreaded evil red eye. Far off in the distance, a fire line could be seen, but that was on Circle A. Against the push of the wind, the fire was retreating instead of advancing. Cal was damned sorry for the Circle A. They could lose a lot of acres, but right now he was too weary to even think about it.

He wasn't sure his legs would carry him back to the chuck wagon. His face was soot smeared, and his hands were blackened. There were a few more holes in his shirt where other sparks had dropped on him, but he had seen and extinguished them before they did much damage. Good God, he was so tired. He could go to sleep tonight and not wake up for a solid year.

Cal filled his plate with food at the chuck wagon and found a small tree bole to put his back against. Without the tree's support he was too weary to sit upright.

Cal tasted his food, and his face twisted with disgust. The beef was tough and almost cold. The beans were burned, the fried potatoes on the raw side. He spat out the food with no real resentment. He was too tired to eat anyway. He took a swallow of coffee and spewed it out. Damned if Briscoe hadn't warmed over the coffee instead of making fresh.

Pardee came over to Cal, and he was boiling mad.

Good, Cal thought. Maybe Pardee had tasted some of the food Briscoe insisted upon calling a meal.

"Who shot those two steers?" Pardee asked heatedly.

"Longbraids and me," Cal answered. "The drags wore out. We had to have something to take their place."

"I guess that damned Indian suggested that," Pardee growled

Cal looked evenly at him. Pardee was a prejudiced man. Once he got something lodged in his mind, it took dynamite to blast it out.

"He did," Cal said quietly.

"You do a lot of listening to him," Pardee said hotly. "First, those fire drags, then all those Indians. Am I supposed to pay them?"

"You sure as hell are." The heat in Cal's voice matched Pardee's. "What in the hell is the matter with you? He saved you a lot of grief today. Maybe he even saved your steers. And you're still picking on him."

That stung Pardee, for Cal could see the flush in his face.

"I suppose next you're going to tell me he's the best man on the payroll."

"Damned near it," Cal snapped. A thought appalled him. My God, Pardee wasn't thinking of cutting Longbraids loose, was he?

"If you're looking for somebody worthless, take a hard look at the Briscoes. The three of them aren't worth a nickel."

Pardee's face burned brighter.

Ah, Cal thought in malicious satisfaction. He's tasted Briscoe's food tonight.

Pardee had lost a lot of ground and knew it, but he tried to come back to the attack.

"I suppose you're going to tell me that Indian is a better cook than Deke."

"Any way you look at it," Cal replied. "Don't think I don't know what I'm talking about. Joe did the cooking while we looked over the new lease."

That really set Pardee back hard. Cal could see him search his mind for a fitting reply.

"I'll tell you one thing," Pardee finally said in triumph. "Your Indian isn't worth a damn with a rope."

He stalked off, completely pleased with himself.

Cal couldn't keep from grinning, and he laughed softly. Even when Pardee was dead wrong, he wouldn't stop until he found something no matter how ridiculous it was, to prove he wasn't wrong.

Cal admitted that Longbraids wasn't the best with a rope, but then he hadn't been born with one in his hands. All Longbraids needed was more time and experience.

Cal looked at Pardee moving away and without any malice in his voice muttered, "You hardheaded, old bastard."

Chapter Thirteen

THE SUMMER SLIPPED by so quickly that Cal didn't realize it was almost gone until he looked up at the sky and saw long V's of geese and the tighter masses of ducks winging their way southward. They knew winter was just around the corner. Cal sat in the saddle a long time, watching the birds. The sad-sweet cry of the geese drifted down to them, and the felt a nostalgia he had known before. It stirred a vague longing in him, one that he could never explain. Maybe it was because the birds were completely free, and he was earthbound.

He looked around. Longbraids was watching him. Cal grinned faintly. "Daydreaming, Joe. I should have know they'd be leaving soon. The mornings are getting nippy."

Longbraids nodded soberly. "They're leaving earlier than usual," he said. "Could mean a long, hard winter."

Cal accepted the observation without objection. Longbraids kept looking up at the sky. He had something important on his mind but was having trouble putting it into words.

"Say it, Joe," Cal said gently.

"Maybe it's past time for Pardee to start his fall roundup," Longbraids suggested. An early winter could catch us before we're through."

Cal was in complete agreement. He had mentioned the same possibility to Pardee a couple of weeks ago, but Pardee hadn't even listened. The steers were daily putting on pounds, and Pardee wanted them to keep on gaining as long as possible.

"I'll talk to him, Joe," Cal replied. He wouldn't bet on his success, but a few times in the past, he had been able to change Pardee's mind.

They sat together, watching the flocks go over, bound together by kindred thinking. It had been a busy summer for both of them. Cal had asked for Longbraids to assist him in the gentling of the rough string of horses, and Pardee had reluctantly consented. Cal grinned faintly as he recalled Pardee's acid remark about Longbraids not being able to handle a rope. The remark still might be half true, but Cal couldn't have picked a better man. Cal still believed he was the best rider in the outfit, but Longbraids was gaining on him fast. Longbraids' mastery of Troublemaker had given him the assurance he needed; the other rough ones were only minor problems.

Cal was proud of their accomplishment. There were only five horses left in the rough string, and he wouldn't berate himself or Longbraids, if those five never gentled down. The D bar S had the best remuda Cal would ever see. Every one of them carried their heads low and moved as quietly as a cat. Pardee couldn't find a single flaw in Cal's and Longbraids' work. There wasn't a single high-headed horse in the remuda, and all of them worked without a lot of fuss. Pardee would further appreciate not having mounts that snorted, threw their heads, or fought the bit when the roundup started. Cal had seen many a devil-raising horse like that spook a roundup and scatter the gather all over. Those kind of horses caused a lot of work to be done over, and they were harder on their riders.

"I'll go in and talk to Pardee now," Cal said.

Longbraids must have recognized the heaviness in Cal's tone. He grinned, "I wouldn't have your job for the world," he said.

To Cal's surprise, Pardee listened to him and nodded agreement. Cal wished he could have asked for one other thing—a new and competent cook. But that would be pushing Pardee too far.

The long hard days of work started the following day. Reps from a dozen cattle outfits rode in to help with the gather, to find any brands of their individual outfits, and turn them back on their proper ranges. It made the work easier, but it didn't shorten the days.

Each timbered draw and river bottom rough land had to be combed for the animals Pardee wanted to ship. A cowboy didn't know when an animal would suddenly break out of the cutbank windbreaks. Then the chase started, usually a long one before the animal was convinced he had to go another way.

The buttes had to be searched. The silvery leafed, thorny buffaloberry thickets were the worst of all. A man rode into one of those thickets at considerable risk to his clothes and skin.

Slowly the gather grew. Cows and calves and younger steers were turned back to graze for another year. Pardee never said a single word of approval, but Cal caught the gleam in his eyes. This shipment was going to be good. Pardee was beginning to see a light at the end of a long dark tunnel.

Longbraids was as taciturn as Pardee, but Cal knew the Indian was pleased by the condition of his own cattle. Longbraids wanted his marketable cattle thrown in with Pardee's shipment.

"I lied to you, Cal," Longbraids said as he stretched out beside Cal after a long hard day. "I told you I had nearly two hundred head. The tally shows that I have two hundred and twenty-four head carrying my brand."

"Good for you," Cal said heartily.

"Will Pardee carry my grazing bill until I get to market?" Longbraids looked anxiously at Cal.

"You know he will," Cal assured him. Just the same he felt some of Longbraid's uneasiness. If Pardee bucked over this arrangement, Cal was going to pound knots on his head.

Cal arose abruptly and said, "I want to talk to Pardee."

He grunted as Longbraids said, "Good luck, Cal."

Cal shook his head as he walked away. He wasn't fooling that damned Indian for a minute. Longbraids knew what Cal wanted to talk over with Pardee.

Pardee listened to what Cal had to say, then nodded absently. He was too pleased with the size of the gather of steers to find something to pick at now.

"Maybe we missed a few," Pardee said. "Oh well. We'll get them next year."

Cal nodded. It was virtually impossible to gather every single animal. A few of those old mossy horns slipped through, fighting to the very last the prospects of being driven from their familiar range. That was why in every roundup five and six-year old steers, or even older animals always showed up.

"Good God," Pardee said explosively. "I've been riding the ragged edge all my life. For the first time, I feel like I've moved away from that edge. It feels good."

He threw his arm awkwardly across Cal's shoulders in a rare display of sentiment. "We start the drive to the ferry in the morning. Hell son. Everything's going to be all right."

"I know," Cal said. He stood quietly beside Pardee, thinking of the last time he had talked to Hale. Lord, it had been longer than he realized. He wondered if Hale had acquired an interest in that ferry. Probably, he thought; with all that drive Hale had in him. He didn't dare mention it to Pardee. That stubborn cuss might choke if he heard that piece of news.

Cal felt a touch of moisture on his cheek and lifted a hand to wipe it away.

"That felt like a snowflake," he commented. "Good thing we're ready to start now. A bad snowstorm—" Cal shook his head and didn't finish the dire statement.

Nothing could dampen Pardee's spirits now. He looked up at the heavy lowering clouds and said positively, "You're imagining things. It ain't going to snow. Nothing bad can happen now."

Cal hoped Pardee was right, but just the same he wished it was Longbraids making that prophecy and not Pardee.

Pardee looked at the group of men clustered around the chuck wagon. "Looks like they're not being fed," he said angrily. "You better get over there and see what's holding Deke up."

Cal nodded and walked toward the chuck wagon. Briscoe was usually late with his meals. That was the best thing that could happen to his food, Cal thought sourly.

"What is it, Duff?" Cal asked as he came up to Granger.

"You ask them," Granger said, pointing to Jude and Dent. "Deke's not around, and nothing's ready. Goddammit, Cal. All of us are hungry."

"I'll take care of it," Cal said. He approached Jude and Dent. Neither of them would look at him.

"Where's Deke?" he asked coldly.

The two stole little glances at that angry face, then looked hastily away. "He's sick, Cal," Dent said. "Real bad. He's got an ache in his belly. We're real worried about him."

He's probably drunk, Cal thought in disgust. "Where is he?" he snapped.

"Lying down," Jude replied. "All he needs is a little rest. He's been working so hard he's plumb worn out."

Cal stared at the two, his eyes blazing. He felt both of them were lying. He could demand to know where Briscoe was, but Jude and Dent would lie to protect their father. At best, they would delay Cal every way possible, hoping that Briscoe would recover and sneak away. Cal wanted nothing better than to kick the tarnations out of Deke Briscoe, but that satisfaction could wait. The important thing now was to see that the men were fed.

"Either of you cook?" he demanded.

Jude and Dent shook their heads, and disgust

mounted in Cal's face. Neither of them was worth a damn.

"You can get a fire started, can't you?" Cal yelled. He started to move away, then paused. "That fire better be going by the time I get back."

Cal heard the angry mutterings of the men clustered around Granger, and he paused long enough to say, "Hold it down. You'll get a meal."

Maybe Longbraids wouldn't want to assume the duties of cook and maybe it was too much to ask, but Longbraids was Cal's only out.

"Joe," he said as he came up to Longbraids. "I'm in a bad bind. Briscoe's missing and neither Jude nor Dent can cook."

Longbraids immediately got to his feet. "Sure, Cal. But it might be worse than the stuff Briscoe has been turning out."

"I've eaten your cooking Joe. I'm satisfied. If you handle this, I owe you again, Joe."

"No you don't," Longbraids said decisively. "When you get an Indian satisfied, you've done something." He started toward the chuck wagon, then said, "Give me about an hour, Cal."

"Sure," Cal said. Just let that hardheaded Pardee try to say something against Longbraids to him.

Chapter Fourteen

LONGBRAIDS DIDN'T NEED all of the hour he asked for in preparing the meal. Cal stood at the end of the line of men moving slowly toward the chuck wagon. Granger was ahead of him, sniffing at the savory aroma.

"I'll say one thing," he said. "It smells damned good."

Longbraids loaded Granger's plate with slabs of steak that didn't have the life fried out if it, and heaped fried potatoes beside them. He had prepared gravy, and Longbraids asked Granger, "Want gravy?"

"Pour it on," Granger said delightedly.

Longbraids filled a cup with coffee, and Granger, both hands occupied, moved away to find a place to sit down.

Longbraids filled a plate for Cal. "I hope it's all right." He couldn't keep the note of anxiety out of his voice.

"Listen to them," Cal said. "That should tell you everything."

The men, already eating, swore happily between mouthfuls.

"There's only one thing you have to worry about now," Cal said. He grinned at the concern in

Longbraids' eyes. "You better hadn't run out. They'll sure as hell be back for more." That was another glaring fault with Briscoe; he served such skimpy meals. Cal could swear that Briscoe acted as though the cost of feeding the hands came out of his own pocket.

Longbraids smiled. "I cooked plenty," he said.

Cal picked up his plate and cup. "I'll take this to Pardee, then come back for mine. Don't you let those wolves beat me out."

"I won't," Longbraids promised.

Cal took the cup and plate to Pardee, then returned for his own food. By the time he sat down beside his father, Pardee's cup was half empty.

"How's the food?" Cal asked casually. By the inroads Pardee had made on his plate it must be good. Cal took a swallow of his coffee while he waited for Pardee to answer.

"Pretty good coffee," Pardee admitted.

"Good?" Cal exploded. "You haven't tasted coffee this good for so long you've forgotten how it's supposed to taste."

"Food's not bad, either." Pardee grinned sheepishly.

Cal busied himself eating for a long while. "Then tell him," he grunted, motioning toward Longbraids.

He doubted that Pardee would ever do that. Getting a compliment out of Pardee was harder than pulling teeth.

Pardee scraped his plate clean, then asked in an offhand way, "I wonder if he's got any left."

"He has," Cal said. "You'd better get a move on. Some of the men have already come back for seconds."

"I still say he's a damned poor roper," Pardee said fiercely before he started toward the chuck wagon.

That hardheaded old bastard. Cal laughed until the tears came to his eyes. Longbraids could be dressed in an angel's robes, and Pardee would still fault him for poor roping.

Cal returned for his second plate of food. "Did Pardee tell you how much he enjoyed his supper?"

"He said it was pretty good," Longbraids said dolefully.

"Hell, that's heaping praise for him," Cal said. "You about through, Joe?"

"I've got to clean up," Longbraids replied. "Things were in quite a mess."

Cal nodded. "I know." He didn't give a damn what happened to Briscoe. D bar S had a cook.

Cal fell asleep watching Longbraids work. Good Lord, wouldn't he ever stop? The last thing Cal remembered was seeing Longbraids start toward the creek for two more buckets of water.

Cal didn't know what awakened him, some sound or an instinct that said something was wrong. He sat up, listening. He had no idea of how long he had been asleep, but Longbraids should have returned by now.

Cal listened intently. That sounded like a scuffle of some kind at the creek.

He threw off his blankets, pulled on his boots, and stood. He had no idea what that scuffle was, but knew he better investigate.

As he approached the creek, Cal saw the heaving, threshing mass on the ground. "You goddamned Indian," he heard Dent say. "Lie still. We'll show you, you can't take our Pa's job."

Jude had Longbraids' arm stretched out on the ground, while Dent held the other. Longbraids tried to throw them off, but he seemed dazed and confused. His usual strength was missing.

Briscoe advanced toward the three figures on the ground, a knife blade gleaming in his hand. "Hold him still," he said shrilly. "I'll cut his damned braids off."

Cal went blind with rage. That would be one of the greatest indignities Longbraids could suffer. Cal roared and rushed forward, swing a fist at the end of the last stride. Dent turned a startled face toward him, and Cal smashed him in the face. The force of the blow lifted Dent and knocked him over backwards. He lay there, clawing at his bleeding face and moaning softly.

Cal whirled on Jude. Jude was coming up from his crouch, and Cal tried to kick his head off. Jude's head snapped back, jerking his body with it. He landed on his back, his face turning red under the rush of blood. He lay there, not a sound or a movement coming from him.

"Why, goddamn you," Briscoe squawked. "You can't do that to my boys."

"I just did," Cal said savagely.

Briscoe advanced toward Cal, making little circles with the knife's point. "I'm going to open you up wide," Briscoe spat as his face contorted and twin streams of saliva ran down from his lip corners.

Cal cursed himself for not having his gun with him. Briscoe's eyes were glazed, and he mouthed obscenities.

Cal retreated before Briscoe's advance, keeping

a wary eye on that knife point. He would kick the hell out of Briscoe, if he just had the chance.

Twice, Briscoe rushed him, and Cal jumped back, sucking in his belly and throwing up his arms to avoid the slashing knife. The third time, Briscoe was quicker. Instead of slashing at Cal's stomach, Briscoe ripped at one of Cal's upflung arms, and Cal's teeth locked at the sudden whip of pain on the inside of a forearm. That knife point had nicked him good.

Cal backpedalled rapidly, and Briscoe's cackle of laughter twisted his face. "That's just a sample, boy. Before I'm through, I'm going to cut you in little pieces."

"What the hell is going on here?" Pardee roared.

Cal felt limp with relief. The noise must have awakened Pardee, too. Thank God. Pardee would stop Briscoe with the rifle he carried.

"They were manhandling Longbraids, Pa. I took care of those two on on the ground, but Briscoe had a knife."

"Why, goddamn him, he cut you," Pardee said, the fury making his words run together.

Cal rubbed his forearm. It was bleeding freely, the blood making it look worse than it really was, but it stung like hell.

"He came pretty close, Pa," he admitted.

"Drop that knife, Deke," Pardered ordered. His face was livid with passion. "I said drop it."

"We were just having a little fun with the Indian," Briscoe complained. "Cal didn't have any right to do what he did."

Pardee pulled the trigger, and a little geyser of

dirt spurted up around Briscoe's feet. "You're thickheaded, Deke," Pardee said coldly. "I won't tell you again."

Briscoe still wasn't convinced. "Pardee," he cried. "You're forgetting what I did for you."

"No," Pardee corrected. "I remembered for far too long. You've got a couple of seconds." He shifted the rifle muzzle until it was centered on Briscoe's belly. "Any way you want it, Deke."

Briscoe's hand opened and the knife fell to the ground. His face was breaking up, and Cal thought he would bawl.

"This ain't fair, Pardee. Not fair at all."

"Get those two on their feet." Pardee jerked the rifle barrel toward Dent and Jude. "And get out of here."

Briscoe looked as though he was stricken. "Pardee, you can't mean that."

"I better hadn't find you on my land in the morning," Pardee said ominously. "Get on your horses and get."

Briscoe made one last effort. "Pardee, you haven't paid us yet. You can't just kick us out without—"

"Shut up," Pardee roared. "I paid you three a week ago. I figure you Briscoes have dogged it more than a week's wages. The bill is settled. Both ways."

Pardee and Cal stood together, watching Briscoe get his two sons on their feet.

The three shuffled off into the darkness, and Pardee said, "I should've seen it a long time ago. But I kept thinking—" He shook his head and didn't finish.

Cal didn't comment. That was as close as Pardee could come to admitting he was wrong.

Longbraids sat up, the dazed look still on his face. He shook his head several times as though he was trying to clear it.

Cal helped him up. "You all right, Joe?"

"All right," Longbraids mumbled. "One of them crept up behind me and hit me with something." He kicked at a short length of a thick tree branch. "Maybe that's it."

His eyes widened as he looked at the blood dripping from Cal's arm. "He cut you."

"Just nicked the skin," Cal said easily. "It looks worse than it is."

Longbraids pulled a handkerchief from his pocket and insisted upon wrapping up Cal's arm. He looked up once and said quietly, "Don't you ever say anything again about you owing me anything."

"If you two are sure you can stay out of trouble for the rest of the night, I'm going back to bed." Pardee stomped off, his shoulders a stiff line.

"I never thought I'd see the day when he'd fire the Briscoes," Cal said in small wonder.

"You know why," Longbraids pointed out. "He couldn't stand the thought of his son being cut."

"Maybe," Cal replied. "Maybe he didn't like seeing the best cook he's had in a long time, being kicked around."

They stood there, grinning at each other in another shared experience.

Longbraids looked at Pardee's retreating figure, and said reflectively, "A tough man. I hope it ends here."

"It's done," Cal replied.

"I don't know," Longbraids said dubiously. "The Briscoes won't forget this."

Cal refused to let Longbraids' words bother him. This time, Longbraids was wrong. "We won't see them again," Cal said positively and followed Pardee.

Chapter Fifteen

SEVERAL OTHER OUTFITS had arrived ahead of the D bar S so there was an additional five-day delay at the ferry.

Pardee cursed that delay with all the passion in his being. Cal wondered again if Hale had bought an interest in the ferry and winced as he thought, if he has and Pardee hears about it, he will literally explode. Cal knew he would blame Hale for every minute of the delay.

Pardee came up to Cal and said, "I guess we're next. I'd like to see the man who runs this scow. By God, I'd tell him what a miserable operation he's running."

Don't show around here now, Hale, Cal prayed. He looked up at the sky to keep Pardee from reading his face.

"What are you looking up there for?" Pardee asked. He sounded as though it was a personal affront to him. "I told you it wasn't going to snow, didn't I?"

Cal wanted to say, I forgot God checks with you before he lets anything happen, but held the remark. In the mood Pardee was in, crossing him now would be like running your hand down a sleeping bear's throat. Anything that happened to you from then on was your own fault.

But Cal sympathized with Pardee. They were so close to getting this shipment over with and done. Pardee had to be dying inwardly in fear that some calamity might happen.

Cal waited until Pardee moved away before he looked up at the sky again. It could snow at any time; this was early November, and clouds had hung around for over a week. Pardee had refused to admit it, but they were damned lucky to get this far without a hard snow hampering them.

It took a little over five ferry loads to get the steers across the river. The animals had handled easier than Cal could remember. Not even a minor break had marred the drive to the river. Of course, all the weight the steers had gained was helping too. A fat steer was less likely to run than a lean one.

The steers were driven off the ferry and through the long lane fenced with eight feet high snow fences. The lane led into the shipping pens. Each pen had its own loading chute, leading to the stock car's loading level. Ten cars could be spotted at a time.

The loading proceeded quickly. It took an hour to load a train with four hundred head of steers, but the railroad handled its business well and swiftly, moving the loaded train out and a new one in with scarcely a delay. Pardee assigned a man to ride each of the six trains. At every stop the train made, the assigned man would go through the cars, seeing that the feed bunks along one side of each car were replenished with hay. They would spot the downed animals and try to get them back on their feet. If they couldn't and the animal died, it was tossed off the train. There would be some losses; there always were.

The men Pardee picked grinned broadly at the assignment; except Granger.

"Big picnic to them," Granger said disconsolately. "But they're young. They don't know how far it is to Chicago."

Cal nodded his understanding. One of those trips was enough in a man's lifetime. He grinned and said, "Look at all the fun you'll have in Chicago."

"Sure." Granger's mood didn't lighten. "I'll wind up spending my money on some woman I won't be able to remember and it'll take the return trip for me to get my head back to normal size."

Cal laughed and slapped him on the shoulder.

He stood with Pardee and the others, watching the last train pull away. Hit a good market, he prayed.

Pardee was in an expansive mood. "Tonight's on me," he bellowed.

The remaining riders whooped their approval. "What are we standing around here for," Pete cried. "Let's get going."

They surged away together, laughing and mauling each other in high spirits.

Pardee noticed Cal and Longbraids hadn't moved, and he frowned at them. "Didn't you hear me? I said tonight's on me."

Wakeman's was the biggest saloon in town, and Cal was afraid Pardee would head for it. Hale could readily be there, and Cal didn't know how a meeting between Pardee and Hale would turn out. He wanted to tell Hale that Pardee was in town. After that what happened was Hale's business.

"We'll be along later, Pa," Cal said easily.

Pardee snorted his displeasure and stomped away.

Cal waited until his father was out of earshot. "Didn't you want to go, Joe?" he asked.

Longbraids shook his head, a slow, decisive gesture. "Sometime during the evening, all the fun will vanish. Somebody will take a remark wrong, then trouble starts. No, it is no place for me."

Longbraids sounded as though he had been through such experiences before, and Cal sympathized with him. Maybe Longbraids knew nothing but trouble could result from mixing an Indian with free flowing whiskey.

"Sure, Joe," he said gently.

It was beginning to snow hard; large lazy flakes floating to the ground.

"A bad winter," Longbraids said positively. "Before it is over the river will freeze solid. Another month, and we won't need the ferry. We can ride over the ice."

"I want you to meet my brother, Joe," Cal said. "Let's get out of this damned snow." He didn't attempt to explain at the faint surprise that appeared in Longbraids' eyes. Neither Pardee nor Cal had mentioned a brother.

Cal knew relief as he saw the light in Hale's office. Hale was working late. At least, he wouldn't be in Wakeman's when Pardee walked in.

He walked into the office and said, "Hale, I want you to meet Joe Longbraids. The best man Pardee ever hired."

Hale wrung Longbraids' hand with enthusiasm. "Cal did some talking about you after he came back inspecting the lease. Cal and Pardee are lucky to have you."

Longbraids smiled faintly. "Cal exaggerates," he said, but Cal could see that he was pleased.

"Pardee's in town," Cal announced abruptly. "He was heading for Wakeman's."

Distress momentarily touched Hale's face, then it was gone, leaving his face untroubled. "Good," he said. He added mischievously, "He won't know that in a way he's contributing to my support."

Cal sighed. The animosity between them was as strong as ever. The Deckers still had two hardheaded people in the family.

"We just finished shipping six trainloads of cattle," Cal said as he sat down.

Hale waved Longbraids to another chair and pulled out the special bottle and three glasses from a drawer. There was no hesitancy in his manner as he filled a glass and handed it to Longbraids. Cal appreciated that.

"I'm glad the fall roundup was good," Hale said and meant it. That mischievous note crept back into his voice again. "I bought into the ferry. Your using it means more dollars to me."

"Don't ever mention that to Pa," Cal warned.

"Lord no," Hale said hastily.

They sat there for a pleasant two hours, occasionally sipping at their drinks. Not once had Hale mentioned Ellie, probably because Longbraids was here. Cal wanted to ask about her, and a faint hope sprang to life within him. Maybe there had been a quarrel. But Cal refused to add fuel to the hope. Ellie and Hale weren't that stupid.

"Gotta be going," Cal said and rose.

Hale walked to the door with them. He wrung Longbraids' hand again and said, "Joe, drop in anytime you're in town. Cal knows he's welcome."

He hesitated a long moment, then blurted out, "Cal, I'm getting married in the spring. Yes, it's Ellie." He watched anxiously for Cal's reaction.

"Fine," Cal said heartily. Even to himself, his voice rang true. "Couldn't happen to two nicer people." The hope was all dead now.

"I like him," Longbraids said as he and Cal walked down the street.

"We're a hell of a lot closer now than we used to be," Cal said. "We were always fighting. Hale always believed he could whip me." And you did whip me Hale, in the only fight that was important, Cal thought mournfully.

"Fighting between brothers always happens," Longbraids said thoughtfully. "It doesn't mean anything. They grow up and forget about it. The bad fight is between father and son. That one is never forgotten."

"Yes," Cal said abruptly. He didn't want to talk about it. Longbraids had a keen perception.

Chapter Sixteen

THAT FIRST SNOWSTORM wasn't the only punch nature had in her bag. One snowstorm followed another, but the cattle were surviving fairly well. They crowded into the draws and ravines and packed the creek and river bottoms where the thickets were the densest. They found not only protection from the wind, but the snow didn't deepen there as it did out in the open. The cattle would find enough forage to keep them going, unless the winter worsened. That 'unless' drove Cal wild. He was in the saddle day after day, checking constantly on the huddled bunches of cattle.

Each night, he had another distressing report to add to the ones he had already given Pardee. "Four more, Pa," he said wearily. "The weakest ones are lying down and dying. I guess they're too tired to struggle any more. I had to shoot two of them." He thought there was accusation in Pardee's eyes and said in defense, "They would never get up. Wasn't it kinder to put them out of their misery? His voice picked up heat. "Dammit, Pardee. We never got through a winter without winter kill. Even in Texas."

Pardee shook his head wearily, and Cal realized his eyes were haunted, not accusing. "I'm not blaming you for anything, Cal. But it's coming so early and so hard. Hell, we're not out of December yet.'' That gray pallor had returned to his face, and he stared blindly across the room. "Once they get you down, they never let you up."

Cal knew who Pardee meant by 'they'. It was everything rolled into one great burden until a man staggered under the load.

"Maybe it'll get better, Pa."

Pardee flung him a bitter glance. That hadn't been any consolation to him at all.

Longbraids rode with Cal in the morning. Both men had their chins buried into the collars of their sheepskins against the merciless onslaught of the wind.

"Temperature's dropping," Cal remarked.

Longbraids looked at the sky and gloomily shook his head.

"Don't say it," Cal yelled. He couldn't stand another dire prophecy.

The full force of the storm arrived before they could get back to the house. The howling gale drove snowflakes into Cal's face until his skin burned under the onslaught.

The depth of the snow had grown appreciably before they got the horses under shelter and unsaddled. Cal and Longbraids plowed toward the house, their heads low as they gasped for breath under the buffeting of the storm.

Oh Jesus, Cal thought bitterly, as Pardee's words came back to him. They were down all right. This South Dakota winter was kicking the hell out of them.

Cal couldn't sit down. He paced the room restlessly, stopping every now and then to stare out a window at a world of white. Visibility was getting poorer by the moment. A few moments ago Cal had been able to make out the hazy outlines of the barn; now it was completely obscured.

Pardee sat across the room, his hands dangling between his knees, his head on his chest. Cal had spoken to him when he came in, but Pardee hadn't replied. Pardee knew how bad the storm was without asking questions.

Every now and then, Cal stepped outside to check on the temperature.

"Dropping fast," he reported in a low voice to Longbraids. He didn't want Pardee to hear him. "It'll be twenty below zero by morning."

Longbraids nodded as though he expected that, and Cal couldn't help resenting Longbraids' complacency.

The riders straggled in one at a time, and Cal's relief that all of them were safe was wiped out with each report the riders gave him. "Getting worse," was the consensus of every report.

Longbraids was out in the kitchen, and the clatter of pans attracted Cal. He walked into the kitchen and asked, "What do you think you're doing?"

"Getting supper," Longbraids replied briefly.

Cal couldn't help his flare of temper. "Who's thinking of food now?"

"A man's got to eat, hasn't he?" Longbraids asked practically.

Cal stared helplessly at him. Longbraids' acceptance of enduring whatever happened outraged Cal. Sure, he realized it was the only thing a man could do, and maybe it was the best way. But dammit— Cal turned abruptly before any more hot words poured out of his mouth.

The storm lasted well into the third day. Some of the windows banked up so high with the snow that it was difficult to tell day from night. If anything, the wind strengthened, and it howled around the house. The house shook with each fierce blast.

Cal wore himself out with his restless pacing, but Longbraids' stoic acceptance never changed. Cal had to keep firm control of himself to avoid railing at him.

Longbraids cocked his head to one side and listened. "Wind's died."

Cal nodded glumly. He was well aware of that. After the howling of the wind, the silence was almost equally hard to bear.

"Let's go out and see how bad it is," Cal said.

He donned all the clothes he could put on and still be able to move.

He walked outside, and the first step carried him into a drift over waist high. This was the final outrageous touch, and Cal cursed the drift until he was breathless. Longbraids never said a word. He just stood there and waited for Cal to run out of breath.

They waded to the barn through snow knee high, and it didn't take much of that kind of effort to put an ache in a man's calves. Cal didn't curse the snow any more, though he was still stiff with indignation at Longbraids' censure. Dammit, didn't a man have a right to curse anything?

Longbraids was behind Cal, and he touched him on the shoulder. "Look," he said.

Cal turned as Longbraids pointed at some thirty

head of cattle. They shuffled along, their heads hanging low, every now and then, bawling mournfully. Cal knew that bawl. These were hungry, miserable animals.

Cal stared at Longbraids. Why had he pointed out this particular bunch of cattle? They would look no worse than any other bunch they would see today. Their backs were plastered under a thick coating of snow and ice, extending over their heads and faces. These were starving cattle. Already, their bellies were shrunken, though the thin tracery of their ribs and the sharpness of their backbones were not yet apparant. That would come very soon, if these cattle couldn't find feed.

"Look at their brands," Longbraids said softly.

As the cattle slowly filed by, Cal looked at one brand, then a second. It didn't hit him until he looked at the third brand. These were all Circle A cattle.

Cal stood stunned by an idea that was beginning to hit him hard. Sure, now and then, other brands strayed onto D bar S land. In the roundup of the steers, they had cut out dozens of foreign stock. But that had been only a simple matter of shoving them back where they belonged. Cal wasn't trying to delude himself there were no more foreign brands around, but surely there wouldn't be as many as this.

"My God, Joe," he said hating to put into words what he was thinking. "This means that the fences are drifted over."

Longbraids nodded somberly. "And the ravines are level full."

Cal stared at Longbraids appalled. If the fences

were snowed under, and the natural barriers were rendered ineffective, it meant that cattle could roam at will. They would drift southward, following their instincts. The three million acres of Indian land would turn into one vast pasture. Cal's head rocked at the thought of all the cattle on the reservations being thrown into one vast herd. When spring finally came, it would mean one huge roundup that would surpass all others.

"My God, Joe," Cal said again, unable to put into words the enormity of what now faced them. In a shaking voice, he added, "I better go back in and tell Pardee."

D bar S riders were in their saddles throughout the day, trying to learn the extent of the disaster. They came upon bunch after bunch of cattle, and not all of them were D bar S.

Cal had never heard of some of the brands, and Longbraids said in a low voice, "They came from a long way off."

Again Cal's head reeled with what was ahead of them. Just separating the cattle and getting them back where they belonged was a task that boggled a man's mind. If any of the cattle are alive by spring, Cal thought grimly.

Each day was a long, tortuous nightmare piled upon too many like it. There was really little that man could do, except watch cattle die. All the individual outfits banded together in one common cause, to save as many cattle as they could without regard to the brand they carried. Every day was filled with the sharp cracks of rifle fire. Cal knew too well what those reports meant; he had been doing too much of that shooting himself. When a rider came upon an animal down and too weak to even make an attempt to get up, a bullet was the kindest thing that could be done for it. When he first came upon such an animal, he felt an impassioned anguish but now all of that was drained from him. Now, he could shoot and ride away from a motionless form without showing emotion. A man wouldn't attempt getting a tally of the dead cattle, for his mind rebelled from the gruesome count.

Days ago Cal had given up the futile effort of swearing. There was no relief in that. He just rode, doing what pitiful little he could to save another head. Pardee never spoke any more, and the gray in his face deepened and remained there like a permanent stain.

The cattle ate anything they could find. They even ate downed timber, if the branches weren't too large to chew through. They striped the underbush and the tree branches they could reach; anything to fill those empty bellies.

The horses did better. They stayed on the ridges, pawing down to grass and found something to put into their bellies. Their coats grew longer and shaggier, and after a while, Cal quit worrying about them. They were going to get through, but the cattle were an entirely different matter.

Some of the mossy horned old steers learned what the horses were doing and quickly moved in after the horses cleared a patch of grass. They used their horns to hook the horses off, and the horses moved to another spot. But there was only a handful of cattle with that much wisdom. The others huddled in the river and creek bottoms, avoiding the bone chilling wind that never seemed to stop.

Riders tried to drive them up onto the exposed ridges where the wind swept the snow away, but the cattle were unable to stay there long. The numbing wind soon drove them back to the bottoms.

Axmen worked day after day, felling small trees, and the cattle devoured the bark and twigs as quickly as they fell. The damned cold deepened day after day, until the small tree trunks froze solid. An ax bounced off them, instead of cutting through. It was like hitting an iron pole with the blade, and the shock of the blow raced through a man's arms and slammed into his shoulders. But their efforts never lessened. Everybody knew cattle couldn't live on such forage, but what else was there?

December limped into January, and Cal thought the storms would never end. The indignity of what they had already suffered was increased by other storms. It was a wonder that men didn't raise their faces to the skies and passionately curse God, or maybe not even that small protest was left in them.

Men froze their feet and hands, and were too tired to take another step, yet they doggedly kept on. A hundred times, Cal wondered where they found the spirit for further struggle against such remorseless odds.

Cal stretched out wearily in another strange bunk. It had been so long since he had been home that he had forgotten what his own bed looked like. This was a common fight and everybody pooled their resources. No longer did a man think only of saving his own cattle; they had all joined the battle to just save a few cattle regardless of whom they belonged to.

Cal winced as the toes of his right foot began to ache. That foot had been badly frostbitten, and Longbraids' quick action had kept Cal from losing toes. Longbraids had insisted upon plunging the frostbitten foot into a tub of snow, and Cal remembered how indignant he had been at such treatment. But it had worked, though for several weeks Cal had been dubious when he looked at the blackened toes. The skin on them had split, but now new skin was forming, though at the end of a long day, that familiar ache came back.

Cal didn't realize that he was rubbing the foot until Longbraids asked from the bunk across from him, "Foot hurt?"

"Some," Cal admitted.

"Soon it will be well," Longbraids said softly. He shook his head, and the gesture said that Cal was one of the lucky ones. Too many men would lose toes and fingers, and others would limp forever.

One last impassioned protest remained in Cal, and he let it out with all the vehemence left in him. "Joe, will this ever end?"

Longbraids took a long time before he answered. He shrugged, then said, "It always has."

The tone of Longbraids' voice scared Cal more than anything else. Before, Longbraids had always been so positive.

Chapter Seventeen

THE PREVAILING WIND picked the direction for the cattle to take. South, always south, the cattle drifted, their heads low as the punishing north wind pushed them on. Cal didn't know how many snow buried fences the cattle crossed. The few times he thought of the massive job that was ahead of everybody to separate these cattle, he always ended up with the grim thought, if any of them survive.

The cattle ate everything that stuck up above the snow, and after bark and twigs, the willow shoots that showed above the snow were a treat.

Every outfit sent riders to trail along with the drifting herds. Cal supposed over a hundred men were engaged in the struggle to save the cattle.

He passed snow covered mounds that marked the spot where cattle had gone down for the last time. The rattle of rifle fire continued to be a constant thing. It sounded like a battle. And it is a battle, Cal thought despairingly, a battle that they were losing. Tomorrow there would be more mounds to add to the mounting total.

Cal guessed he was too numb to feel pity for the suffering animals. The crusted snow had rubbed all the hair off their hocks and legs, and the bleeding had frozen into thin, wavering lines. For the life of him, Cal didn't see how they could keep on going.

The big drift finally wound up in the Little Bend of the Missouri River, somewhere below the Cheyenne River Agency. Everything in its path that was edible was stripped clean. Little ranchers who had put up haystacks against just such a contingency as now hit them, saw the stacks devoured before their despairing eyes. Nothing could stop the onslaught of the starving animals once they smelled or saw the haystack. They ignored every effort to keep them away from the stacks, literally running over men and horses. In a moment, the haystack was surrounded by hungry mouths. In a few more moments, every trace of the haystack was gone.

Cal looked out over the frozen Missouri River with bleak eyes. He had no doubt many of the cattle had drifted on across the frozen river, but there was no thought in anybody's mind of trying to go after them. There were too many thousands of heads packed in the bend.

The cattle's pitiful bawling never stopped, and as long as their strength remained, they milled restlessly. They were only caricatures of their former shapes, and those hollowed eyes seemed more enormous than ever. Their bellies were shrunken under the stark, brutal tracing of their ribs and backbones. Looking at them was enough to drive a man out of his mind.

Cal sat with his gloved hands crossed over the horn, staring over the cattle. He was tired and numb with the cold. He didn't understand a lot of things, and one enormous 'why' pounded like a

great drum in his mind. Why was the instinct to
survive put into creatures? Those cattle had struggled every foot of the way to get here, and this was
only the end of a death march.

Longbraids found Cal and said, "Verl Andrews
has come up with an idea. He wants to build big V
shaped drags, then open paths to the ridges where
the cattle might find feed." He looked at Cal and
asked sharply, "Did you hear me?"

"I heard you," Cal replied. He wasn't indifferent to anything that might save some of the
cattle. He was just too beaten for his mind to
respond quickly. He lifted his hands from the horn
and beat them together to restore a little life into
them. The sharp tingling told him there was still
feeling in them.

"Let's get at it," he said simply.

The V-shaped drags were built of long logs, so
heavy that it took four horses to drag them through
the snow. Cal felt a strong surge of hope as the V
dug into the snow and threw it to either side.
Riders grinned at each other as they looked at the
exposed grass. They couldn't stay on this ridge
long, for the wind was a battering force.

The cattle strongly resisted the efforts to drive
them along the cleared paths. They fought stubbornly with some crazy remaining strength, and
riders ar   orses were exhausted with the effort of
keeping the cattle headed where they should go.

Cal hadn't cursed for sometime, but he cursed
vagely at these blind, stupid beasts. It was almost as though a death wish was implanted so
deeply into their minds that nothing could get it
out.

Step by step, the cattle were forced onto the

heights. All around Cal animals went down and didn't get up again. He hardly heard the occasional rifle shots. He had heard them too often to pay much attention.

Cal was in the group of riders that got the first bunch of cattle onto a rise. The cattle stood there stupidly, their heads close to the exposed grass, but they didn't eat.

"Eat, damn you," Cal raved. His thought of a death wish came back to him. After all this labor, the cattle weren't going to eat.

"Maybe it's been so long they've forgotten how," Longbraids said quietly. "And it's cold up here,"

Cal glared at him. He didn't want any explanations or rationalizations. The damned cattle wouldn't eat.

"Look!" Longbraids exclaimed. "A few of them are nibbling at the grass."

Relief flooded over Cal. All along the ridge cattle had lowered their heads, chewing off mouthfuls of the dried grass. Maybe they were going to save some of the cattle after all.

The relief was wiped away by dismay. The damned stupid things were beginning to wander off the ridge.

"What is the matter with them?" Cal yelled.

Longbraids' tone didn't change. "The wind cuts through them. They are shivering. They no longer have any fat to protect them from the cold. As hungry as they are they prefer the relative warmth of the bottoms."

Cal stared at him slack jawed, momentarily unable to comprehend what Longbraids was saying. "You mean we can only hold them up here as long as we stand guard over them."

"It looks like it," Longbraids said softly.

The days became one long stretch of prolonged agony. After each snowfall the drags opened up new lanes to the ridges, and riders herded cattle along them, holding the cattle as long as human flesh and endurance could stand the biting cold. Cal lost all track of time as one day ran into another. He didn't realize that a man could be so exhausted and still be able to go. Night after night, he was positive he would be unable to get up in the morning, but he did.

He felt he was in some senseless struggle that would never end. But they were getting a little feed into the cattle. He clung to that positive accomplishment. He was quite sure he would have gone mad, if he didn't have that anchor.

Riding back to a bunkhouse, Longbraids pointed at the western sky. "See!" he cried. His voice sounded as though he saw some great glory.

Cal stared dully at the sky. He couldn't see anything outstanding there except for a thickening mass of flat, pancake shaped clouds. That familiar slab of fear raced through him. All those clouds meant to him was that another storm was coming.

"The Chinook winds are coming," Longbraids said, and there was a reverence in his voice. "It is over."

Cal knew what the Chinook winds meant. They would blow their warm breath over the frozen ranges, and the snow would vanish as though by magic. He wanted to believe Longbraids with every fiber of his being, but he couldn't. Even though he had never known Longbraids to be wrong where nature was concerned, Cal couldn't accept his words. The struggle had been too long, too brutal for him to look at the possibility that it could be ending.

"I'll believe it when I see it," he said harshly.

Chapter Eighteen

THE WARM BREATH of the Chinook winds swept over the range. While the snow didn't melt as though by magic, Cal could swear he could see its depth visibly lowering by the hour. The exposed ridges were almost dry before the first day of the Chinook was over, and everytime Cal looked up at them, he could swear the line of snow was pushed farther down to the bottom land. Water was everywhere. Man or horses couldn't take a step without creating a miniature fountain. The creeks ran full, and their voices so long ice locked, now sang a lilting song.

"Do you know what they are singing?" Longbraids asked.

Cal unbuttoned his sheepskin coat. Without the cutting north wind and with the rising temperature, he was uncomfortably warm. He had on too many clothes. Again, he hadn't listened to Longbraids when he said, "You won't need all those clothes today."

As usual Longbraids was right. Cal vowed he would never disagree with Longbraids again. He felt the tension easing out of him, leaving him a spineless blob with no energy to move in a definite direction. The headache of the terrible winter didn't throb so violently, but it was still there, a dull ache in the back of his head. Cal guessed he would carry it for a long time.

He smiled wearily at Longbraids. "No, I don't know what the streams are singing."

He had never seen such a rapt expression on Longbraids' face. Cal had the strange feeling that Longbraids communed with some mystic force he couldn't contact.

"They are singing, spring is coming, spring is coming," Longbraids said simply.

Cal listened to the voice of the waters. The longer he listened, the more he could imagine he heard the refrain, "Spring is coming."

The sound aroused a hostility in Cal. He wasn't arguing with Longbraids about that singing refrain, but it didn't bring him the joy Longbraids expressed.

"It came a little late," Cal said bitterly.

Longbraids shook his head in mild reproof. Cal wasted so much effort assailing the unassailable.

But Longbraids' calm acceptance stirred Cal to violent protest. "Goddamn it," he said harshly. "Show me one good thing that came out of this winter."

"The wolves and coyotes came out of it fat and sleek," Longbraids said. "They will raise big litters this spring."

Cal missed the twinkle in Longbraids' eyes. For a moment, he was so outraged that he was speechless. "I'm in the business of raising cattle," he said hotly. "Not wolves and coyotes." The hostility flowed out of Cal toward Longbraids in almost tangible waves. The only trouble was that it wasn't flowing back; Longbraids was seeking no quarrel.

"Consider that a bad joke," Longbraids said calmly. "I was trying to lift your spirits. I will not be so foolish again."

Cal shrugged, the irritation still with him. He knew very well what Longbraids was trying to tell him. There was that word 'acceptance' again. How could a man accept placidly what had just happened.

He rode along in moody silence. Yes, some of the cattle would live. They no longer had to be driven to the ridges for a few mouthfuls of food before the cold and wind turned them back to the bottoms. All around him cattle were grazing, for the melting snow exposed grass everywhere. It would take a long period of good grazing before the cruelly sharp outlines of the caricatures softened. Some of the weaker ones still wouldn't make it, but most of those on their feet would come through alive.

"Why remember the winter?" Longbraids asked. "The winter is done. The quicker it is forgotten, the better for everybody."

Cal felt his outrage returning. How in the hell could anybody forget these past weeks.

Death was everywhere Cal rode. Longbraids hadn't asked Cal where he was going, but he knew, because he had sighed and turned without speaking. Cal had to torture himself with seeing just how bad their loss was.

Every rushing stream carried dead cattle toward the big river, and along the Missouri the carcasses were lined up as far as Cal could see in both directions. In some places the dead cattle were so thick, a man could walk on the bodies until he was thoroughly weary without every putting a foot on the ground.

Cal rode for a full day, his face growing more grim, his mind reeling with the ghastly extent of the loss. He pulled up his horse abruptly as Longbraids' words came back to him. He wasn't accomplishing a damned thing. Longbraids was right. It was done, and the quicker a man forgot it, the better off he was.

Cal whirled his horse and rode off, never looking back.

The remaining cattle were slowly driven north, never being crowded or hurried. If they could make only a mile or two in a day, then that was it. They needed all the time they could possibily be given to recover some of their strength.

A roundup was held at each fence the vast herd came to. The ones belonging to this outfit's land was cut out and left behind.

At each tally, Cal saw mens' faces pale, then sag into the agony of ruin. Everybody knew the winter kill was horrendous, but the final summary was more frightful than men expected.

The roundup to cut out Pardee's cattle, took a full four days. All the hard riding and the hurry of the usual roundup was missing. Horsemen cut out the designated brand and walked them slowly away from the mass of the main herd.

Now, it was time for Cal to suffer the shock other men had known. His teeth were clenched tightly together, and his face grew whiter and whiter as the D bar S stock was slowly cut out. It wasn't time to even begin to think of a tally, but it was going to be bad, far worse than Cal hoped for.

He knew dully it was only a futile hope, and he shouldn't have tortured himself with better expectations. He had lived with death all around him, and D bar S cattle were no more immune than another brand.

Cal felt somebody watching him and turned his head. Longbraids sat stolidly not thirty feet from his. His face was as impassive as ever, but Cal sensed some kind of a mute plea in his eyes. He nodded briefly with a grimace that was supposed to have been a grin. He turned back to work, cutting out more D bar S brands.

Again, he rode away without looking back. There was more work ahead of him before all the cattle were returned to their proper range. He rode after the dwindling main herd. He had learned one lesson, though it was of little consolation. He hadn't been alone in all this suffering and loss. All these men had been in one leaky boat, and no matter how hard they had tried, they hadn't been able to keep it from slowly sinking.

They stopped briefly to cut out the pitiful remains of the individual Indians' herds. Some of the owners had fewer than two dozen head left.

Cal was sheepishly contrite. He had been so immersed in his own misery that he hadn't even thought of Longbraids' cattle. At the first opportuntiy he would have to ask Longbraids how he fared.

The last bunch of cattle was shoved onto its own range. The big job of separating the herds was done. Cal knew it couldn't possibly be a hundred percent accurate. Here and there a few more alien brands would turn up on strange ranges, but it wouldn't really affect the final total. All that a man could count on was what already in his hands.

Newt Nealey, the foreman of Circle A, paused beside Cal and said, "See you again."

"Not under the same conditions I hope," Cal replied.

"Lord, no," Nealey answered fervently. His grin was twisted, but it was still a grin. "One winter like this is all a man can stand in one lifetime."

Cal watched him canter off, then rejoined Longbraids. "We can go home now, Joe."

Cal kept seeking the proper words to ask Longbraids the dreaded question. He finally gave up and just blurted it out. "I was so occupied in counting D bar S cattle that I completely forgot about yours." A note of apology was in his voice for his negligence. "How bad was it, Joe?"

Longbraids' answer was steady enough. "As near as I can make it, Cal, I lost about seventy-five head."

Cal groaned in sympathy. To a man with a small herd, that was a devastating loss.

Longbraids doggedly shook his head. He wanted neither sympathy nor pity. "I've got more than I started with. The grass will be better this year. It always is after a bad winter."

Cal grunted to cover the heat he felt in his face. Here was another lesson, deftly and softly delivered. A man wasn't through as long as he kept trying.

His laugh was a little forced at first, but it built up until it was free and unrestrained. He could laugh at the funniest thing in the world—himself.

He wiped his eyes and said, "Did I ever get anywhere by arguing with you?"

Longbraids didn't reply, but his eyes were serene.

They rode in silence until the house came in view. Cal shook his head in wonder. "I've been gone so damned long, I guess I expected it to look different.

"Let me have your horse," Longbraids suggested. "Pardee will be waiting to hear from you."

Cal nodded his appreciation, swung down, and handed his reins to Longbraids. He squared his shoulders before he stepped into the house. Telling Pardee the news was going to be the hardest thing he ever did.

He walked into the room, where Pardee sat hunched over in a chair. Cal stood a long moment, staring at him. My God, Pardee seemed to have literally shriveled.

"Hello, Pa," he said quietly.

Pardee's head jerked around, and he stared questioningly at Cal as though he didn't immediately recognize him. Then he sprang to his feet and rushed at Cal. He wrung Cal's hand hard, while his other hand gripped Cal's elbow.

"You and Longbraids get back all right?"

It was a foolish question; Cal was here, wasn't he. "Back okay," he said briefly.

Pardee's eyes searched Cal's face, and he said haltingly, "It was bad, wasn't it?"

"Pure hell," Cal replied.

He watched Pardee struggle to put into words the question he was afraid to ask. "How bad was it?" Pardee finally managed to say.

"We lost three thousand head," Cal said

quietly. "Most of them cows. That total could change by a few head one way or the other." Cal shrugged, knowing that wouldn't really change anything.

Pardee stared at him, his eyes growing bigger and bigger. His face had the grayness of a corpse. Again he struggled to ask something, and Cal saved him that effort. "I'm sure, Pa."

Cal jerked as the sound came from Pardee's lips. At first, it was thin and reedy, then it grew in volume. My God, Pardee was laughing, but it was a sound that had no mirth.

Cal stared in horror. Pardee's mind had cracked under the enormity of this loss. "Pa, stop that!" he commanded sharply.

Pardee choked off that obscene laughter and gasped. "I knew it was bound to happen to me one of these days."

Pardee didn't sound insane. "What do you mean?" Cal asked.

"Why hell, son. I been riding along the ragged edge all of my life. I just fell off of it."

Cal felt mingled relief and distress. That laughter wasn't insanity; it was just a macabre way of looking at the loss.

"Pa, we'll work out of it. The grass will be better this year. Longbraids says—"

Pardee whirled savagely on him. "I don't give a damn what that Indian says. You said most of that three thousand head were cows." Passion was beginning to push a little color into his face. "Don't you see what that means. That was most of our breeding stock. We can't come back after something like that." He was working himself into a rage, but it was better than just numbed acceptance. "All my life I been telling myself that next year would be better. I'm sick of that horseshit."

"There's one thing we can do about," Cal said quietly. "We can just lie down and die."

He left the room, grinning bleakly at the curse Pardee flung after him. That was more like the old Pardee.

Chapter Nineteen

PARDEE WASN'T THE same at all. He shambled about, never speaking even in answer to a direct question. At times, Cal had to repeat a question two or three times before he got a response out of Pardee.

Cal's worry increased daily. Pardee refused to leave the house often, and he absolutely balked at riding out to the cattle. Cal kept saying, "Pa, they're looking better every day. I want to show you—"

Pardee lashed out at him. "I don't want to see those damned cattle. Quit picking at me. You hear me?"

He whirled and stalked away.

Cal watched him with sick eyes. Pardee might look the same on the outside, but that was only a deceptive shell. Inwardly, Pardee was dead.

Cal hesitated a moment, considering whether or not he should tell Pardee he was going into town after supplies, then shrugged in weary resignation. Pardee either wouldn't hear him or would ignore him completely.

To hell with it, Cal thought. He felt no anger, only an overwhelming sadness. Living around a walking dead man was the hardest thing he ever had to bear. If he didn't love Pardee, he wouldn't give a damn.

He got a list of things Longbraids needed for the kitchen and briefly thought of asking if Longbraids had a solution to the problem. He angrily squashed the thought. This was family business. Telling an outsider about it would be like undressing before a crowd.

Cal hitched up the team and drove the wagon toward the ferry landing. He hadn't seen the river for himself, but he had been told the ice was out of the river and the ferry was running again.

The Strip was greening up again, the new delicate shoots of grass pushing stubbornly through the dead grass. He heard birds singing in the distance and felt some understanding about what Longbraids had tried to tell him. Life always returned to this land, if a man had patience enough to endure. Cal could be content, if he could only stop worrying about Pardee.

He stopped in disbelief as the ferry boat came in sight. Somebody was taking cattle across the river at this time of the year. No one would be hunting grass on the other side, Cal reasoned. He was stunned at the obvious reason. The owner was shipping these cattle to market.

The ferry had room for Cal's wagon after the last of the cattle were loaded, and Cal drove aboard. He climbed down, and Dana Edison came over to him.

Cal didn't know Edison too well, for his outfit was at the extreme northern edge of the reservation. Edison was somewhere near Pardee's age, but he looked much older. Cal couldn't remember his hair being so white, either.

Cal shook hands with Edison, and by the slight

frown on Cal's face Edison guessed what he had in mind.

"The last of 'em," Edison said, jerking his head toward the penned cattle. "Shipped four loads yesterday."

"To market?" Cal knew he was babbling like an idiot, but he couldn't help it. He looked at the cattle. They were still pitifully poor, but their eyes were brighter. Regular eating had done that for them. Give them a few more months of good grazing, and they wouldn't be the same animals at all.

"Yes," Edison grimly answered Cal's question.

"My God," Cal burst out. He knew he should have held his words, but he couldn't stop them. "You won't get anything for them."

"I don't give a damn what I get for them" Edison said passionately. "I quit. I wouldn't go through another winter like that for all the cattle in the world."

He felt censure in Cal's eyes, nodded abruptly, and moved away.

Cal felt the sickness coming alive in him again. There but for the grace of God went Pardee. Edison had been whipped beyond the limit of his endurance. Edison didn't know it, but he was a dead man. Letting go was the final act. All he had to do now was to lie down.

Pardee would never go that route, Cal argued with himself. Pardee was too tough to ever be shattered the way Edison was. But remembering those staring, blank eyes in Pardee's hollowed face Cal wasn't so sure. There was never any warning before a man suddenly cracked. Not even a tiny fissure showed to warn of the coming breakdown.

"No," Cal said aloud passionately. That was never going to happen to Pardee.

He fretted all the way across the river. Halfway over, he saw a dozen bobbing cattle carcasses. They were sucked under by the current only to bob up again a few yards in some brush until the rising river lifted and carried them out to mid stream. Damn, Cal was sorry Edison had to see them. It was a brutal reminder of what had happened to every cattleman.

A ferry hand stopped beside Cal at the rail and remarked jocularly, "It's a hell of a lot better. A few weeks ago, the river was packed with them." He pointed at the disappearing bodies. "Whew, the smell. Makes a man gag."

It was clear to Cal that this man wasn't a cattleman. He hadn't suffered the heart-rending losses. The only thing that was important to him was the bad smell that was the aftermath.

"Shut your mouth," Cal said fiercely. "Just keep your damned mouth shut." He glared at the bewildered man and moved away.

"What'd I say?" the man called after him.

Cal was glad when he could drive off the ferry. He had to have somebody to talk to and headed for Hale's office. He stopped before it and tied up his team.

Hale's face brightened at the sight of him. "Been thinking a lot about you," he said. "But I see you got through it all right." He looked at Cal's tight expression and said, "It was pretty rough?"

Cal used the same term he had used before in describing the winter. "Pure hell."

Worry creased Hale's forehead. "Is Pa all right?"

Cal couldn't sit down, and he paced back and forth. "Yes, if you can call it that," he snapped.

"You better tell me about it," Hale said quietly.

Cal whirled and faced him. "We lost three thousand head. Most of them cows."

Hale pursed his lips and whistled softly, though the announcement brought no real surprise to his face. "I was afraid of something like that. How's Pa taking it?"

"Bad," Cal said tersely and went on to describe the incident with Edison. "Edison's quitting, Hale. Selling out, even though he knows he'll get only a fraction of what his cattle will bring later on. I've never seen a more broken man. He doesn't realize if he lets go of everything, he's dead."

At first, Hale couldn't understand what Cal was driving at. "I've heard of others doing the same thing," he said flatly. Then his eyes widened, and he cried, "You're not trying to tell me you're afraid Pa could go the same way?" He scoffed at his own question. "Hell, no. He's too tough."

"You're remembering him the way you last saw him," Cal said. "The change in him would shock you. He sits and stares at nothing for hours at a time." Cal beat his hands together in a frenzy of feeling. "He's a changed man, Hale. I'm telling you he's dead inside."

Hale kept shaking his head, though he didn't deny what Cal said. "What did you have in mind, Cal?" he asked softly.

"I thought you'd ride out and see him. Right

now, it could make the difference."

"Do you think he'd talk to me, even now, Cal?"

For a moment, Cal was furious. It was such a little thing to ask of Hale, but his stiff-necked pride still sought excuses.

The anger faded as quickly as it rose. "No," Cal said heavily. "I guess he wouldn't."

Hale looked at the beaten attitude of his brother and said, "Cal, let me do some thinking about this. Maybe I can come up with something."

"Sure," Cal said and turned toward the door. He should have known it was useless coming here. He couldn't honestly blame Hale. If Cal couldn't do anything when he was right on the grounds, how could he expect Hale to do something?

"I'll see you again, Hale," he said wearily. He didn't turn his head at Hale's 'sure'.

Cal was driving up the street when he remembered he had forgotten to ask about He didn't turn his head at Hale's 'sure'.

Cal was driving up the street when he remembered he had forgotten to ask about Ellie. Dammit, he had an excuse. His mind had been far too filled with other, more important things.

Chapter Twenty

CAL WELCOMED ANY work that came along. Anything was better than sitting in the house watching Pardee brood. Maybe he was worrying too much, perhaps Pardee would snap out of it, but so far Cal hadn't seen the slightest change for the better. He had almost given up trying to talk to his father. Either Pardee didn't hear him, or he didn't want to.

Cal came in from a long, wearying day. The cattle were improving. Cal could swear they were literally putting on pounds every day. He ruefully admitted he was asking for the improbable and knew it was just the rapid improvement that made the change so drastic.

He rode up to the barn, where Longbraids waited for him.

"Don't dismount," Longbraids said. "I want to show you something."

Cal couldn't get anything more out of him despite how many questions he asked. Longbraids had been acting strange the past few days, being gone for long stretches of time. Cal hadn't thought much about it before, but Longbraids' present behavior brought all the wonder back. Cal hadn't the slightest idea what this was all about, but it better be good. He had been in the saddle most of the day, and he didn't appreciate Longbraids adding another ride.

It couldn't be the cattle Longbraids wanted to see, for they were in the opposite direction, almost against the back fence of the lease.

They were headed toward the Strip, and Cal kept glancing at Longbraids as they rode. He couldn't describe the expression on Longbraids' face unless he'd call it a secretive amused little smile. Cal wondered sourly what struck Longbraids so funny.

When they topped this short rise, they woud be within sight of the entrance gate from the Strip. Cal was beginning to get mad. He hadn't seen anything yet that made this ride worthwhile.

He turned his head toward Longbraids. "Joe," he said, "if you're dragging me on some wild goose chase—"

They had reached the top of the rise as Cal spoke. "Look!" Longbraids said, interrupting him. He pointed ahead.

"Oh Jesus Christ," Cal groaned as he saw the cattle. They were strung out all along on the inside of the fence and with their grazing, were beginning to move deeper. All Cal could think of was the work that would be involved in getting them back to their own range; He knew these couldn't possibly be D bar S cattle.

"We must have a hell of a lot of fence down someplace," Cal grumbled. The suspicion flashed across his mind that these cattle had been driven through the gate deliberately, and he discarded it. Nobody would do that for a desperate need of grass. The grass was more than plentiful all over the Reservations.

"Have you seen the brands?" Cal demanded. "Whose cattle are those?"

Longbraids was grinning openly, a happy delight in his eyes. "Yours," he replied. "Yours and Pardee's. Though we're going to have to do a lot of rebranding."

Cal stared at him, astounded. "What the hell are you talking about?"

Longbraids pulled out a thin sheaf of papers from his pocket and handed it to Cal. "Bills of sale, proving those cattle belong to you."

Cal stared at the papers. He could read what was on them, but his mind refused to work. Those papers were legal proof of ownership, and each was signed and dated.

Cal sorted through a half-dozen pieces of papers, each proclaiming that Pardee Decker had just recently purchased these cattle. Something was sadly out of whack here, for Cal knew that Pardee didn't have enough money to buy a dozen head, let alone all the cattle he saw.

A new suspicion was beginning to take form in Cal's mind. "How many cattle are there." He swept a savage gesture at the cattle.

"Three thousand," Longbraids replied. "All cows except a hundred head of bulls, good bulls."

"That damned Hale is behind this," Cal exploded. Now, he knew the reason behind Longbraids' prolonged absences. "And you've been helping him."

"Some," Longbraids admitted. "Though Hale didn't need much help. He knew what he wanted to do. I helped drive them to the gate and push them inside."

"Let's get closer. I want to see them."

Longbraids didn't miss the grim note in Cal's voice, for his eyes were worried.

Cal rode among the cattle, noticing the various brands. All of the cows were thin, but their strength was returning. He was positive he saw calf in several of them. He approved of the bulls he saw, and his thoughts raced ahead to what might be if these cattle were really his. If these cows actually belonged to D bar S, he and Pardee would be back where they were before the winter hit them.

Cal didn't realize he was shaking his head until Longbraids said, "This makes you unhappy?"

"I wish to God they were mine," Cal replied. "But I'm thinking of Pardee. I can just hear him, bellowing his head off when I tell him." Cal minicked Pardee's tone. "By God, I'm not accepting charity from anybody." Cal didn't say the remainder of what was in his mind. "Particularly from an ingrate son."

"No, it won't work, Joe," Cal said decisively.

Longbraids shook his head. "I'll never understand you white men. Hale warned me this might happen. What are you going to do with these cattle?"

"I'm going to tell Hale to take them back," Cal said flatly. "I'm going into town and talk to Hale. If Pardee asks where I am, tell him anything you like." He doubted that as sunk in his misery as Pardee was, he would even notice Cal's absence.

He lifted the reins and started toward the gate. He looked back, and Longbraids was shaking his head. That brought a thin smile to Cal's lips. He could imagine that Longbraids was thinking, these damned crazy white men.

The kerosene lamp was on as Cal walked into Hale's office. Hale's head was bent over some work on his desk, but he heard Cal's entrance, for he lifted his head and grinned.

"Ho, boy," he said. He was in the best of spirits; it showed in his tone and grin.

Hale's face sobered at the foreboding expression on Cal's face, and he sighed. He leaned back in his chair and said argumentatively, "So you know about the cattle? Which one of you doesn't approve? You or Pardee?"

Cal sank down into a chair. "Pardee hasn't seen them yet. I disapprove because I know how he'll react."

Hale's jaw jutted out. "Aren't you jumping to a conclusion? You didn't even talk it over with Pardee," he accused.

"You didn't, either," Cal said quietly. "Pa's pride is about all he's got left. He's looking at himself as a flat failure, and you slap him across the face with something like this. Did you expect him to throw his arms around you."

For a long moment, Hale's eyes darkened, and he breathed hard. Then his resistance collapsed suddenly, and he looked miserable. "Oh, dammit, Cal. I know you're right. All I could think about was getting you two back on your feet. It wasn't such a big thing. It was a buyer's market. I learned long ago to buy on such a market and never sell on a distressed one."

Cal nodded. "That part of your figuring was solid. You just didn't think about Pardee."

Hale's face colored, and he banged his fist on his desk. "Goddammit, Cal. You're saying I should have gone to Pardee first—" He sounded as though he was choking, and he cut off the remainder of his words.

"Something like that," Cal said evenly. "But you couldn't do that. You had your pride to think of."

"Why shouldn't I—" Hale started.

Cal waved him quiet. "If a quarrel is ever going to be settled, somebody's got to give first. Pardee's an old man. His failures hit him harder. Yet you expected him to be the one to give in."

Hale stared down at his desk. "Oh, dammit. I handled it badly, didn't I, Cal?"

"Bad," Cal agreed.

"What am I going to do?" Hale asked helplessly.

Cal's face was grave. "I don't know, Hale."

Hale's face brightened. "If it was up to you, would you take those cattle?"

Cal let out a long breath. "Lord yes, Hale. In a minute. It would be throwing a rope to a drowning man. But I haven't got anything to say about it."

"But you could talk to Pardee, couldn't you?" Hale asked eagerly. "You could make him listen—" He stopped at Cal's shaking head.

"It wouldn't do any good," Cal said gently. "Pardee's retreated so far I can't reach him. I know that this will only shove him farther away."

Hale's face was sick. "I should have gone to him a long time ago and patched things up," he muttered. His grin was twisted as he looked at his brother. "I always was a little thick when it came to seeing things that needed to be done."

"Sure, you were," Cal said in gentle derision. "You've proved that a thousand times over."

That false brightness returned to Hale again. "Cal, couldn't you just keep those cattle around and tell Pardee about it later? In a few months, his spirits are bound to lift."

Cal's chuckle had a sad note. "I would, if you can tell me how I can hide three thousand head of cattle until I think it's the right time to tell Pardee about them."

A dejected look returned to Hale's face. "It wouldn't work, would it? What in the hell am I going to do with those cattle?"

"You've never been stumped for an answer yet," Cal said.

"You eaten yet?" Hale asked abruptly. Cal shook his head and Hale added, "I haven't, either. Let's go get something."

Cal was sure that Hale wanted to talk about this some more. "It won't do any good, Hale," he warned.

"I guess not," Hale said in doleful acceptance. "But we can still eat together, can't we?"

"I'd like nothing better," Cal replied.

While Cal waited for Hale at the door he thought in resignation, Hale will have some more arguments. He never knew Hale to be stopped by one closed door.

As Hale joined his brother, and they stepped outside, Hale paused to roll a cigarette. He wiped a match on his pant leg and bent his head to the flame. Cal had never seen so much distress in a man's face.

Chapter Twenty-one

DEKE BRISCOE TRIED to squeeze another drop out of the whiskey bottle. His face showed disappointment as he looked at the liquid that barely covered the bottom of his glass. He tossed the bottle to the floor and tilted his head far back to get every drop in the glass.

"Hardly more than enough to wet my tongue. Dent, go get me another bottle."

Dent showed his worry. "Pa, can we afford it?"

"Hell, yes, we can afford it," Briscoe roared. He leaned forward, leering at Dent. "We can afford it as long as Jude keeps working."

Dent shook his head, but he got up and walked to the bar. He came back with a bottle and set it before his father.

"Jude ain't going to like it when he walks in and sees this," he said. "He don't like working at the livery stable. He complains it takes every cent he makes to just keep us eating."

"Shut up," Briscoe said savagely. "You just keep your damned mouth shut. You and Jude ain't doing the thinking."

He uncorked the bottle and poured himself a full glass. He rolled the whiskey around in his mouth before he swallowed.

Dent watched his father's Adams-apple bob up and down. Deke's capacity always awed him.

"Man thinks better with a little whiskey in his belly," Briscoe said.

"Pa, when are we going to get out of this town?" Dent begged. "We hung around here all winter and damned near froze our asses off. Hell, there's nothing here for us."

He shrank back before the naked ferocity in Briscoe's eyes.

"I told you a hundred times we're not leaving until I even a score," Briscoe said passionately. "I'm going to show that damned Pardee he can't toss me aside like a worn out boot after all I did for him." He poured another glass, and his hand shook so much from the accumulated fury within him that he spilled some of the whiskey onto the table.

Dent didn't dare look straight at Deke, for fear his father would see the naked dislike in his eyes. He had listened to this tirade so often he was sick of it. He didn't like Pardee any better than Deke did, but Deke was eaten up by his obsession of getting even.

"Dammit, Pa. If you're so set, why don't we just ride out there and take care of him? Let's get it over with."

Briscoe's eyes narrowed to scornful slits. "You've suggested that fifty times. You never learn a damn thing, do you? We ride out there, and we wouldn't get within sight of Pardee. Have you forgotten what he said? Come back, and he'd shoot us. Hell, he wouldn't have to. Any one of his outfit would do it for him."

Dent remembered all that. But just sitting here

wasn't accomplishing a damned thing either. "Are you just going to sit here until he dies a natural death? Would that satisfy you?"

Briscoe slammed his clenched hand on the table so hard that the bottle danced, and the glass overturned. He caught the glass before it rolled off the table.

"Don't give me any of your smart talk," he roared. "You never had any real guts. You let a man walk all over you, and you crawl away without trying to do anything about it.

Dent slumped in weary resignation. "Handle it your own way," he mumbled.

Briscoe poured himself another drink. "You're damned right I will. Because Pardee's never been in town doesn't mean he won't show up here one of these days. When he does, I'll take care of him."

Dent didn't dare let his disgust show on his face. This was the same old talk and nothing would come of it. The one he could burn over was Cal Decker. That bastard had tried to rip his head off. Dent would join in wholeheartedly if Deke was making plans to even the score with Cal Decker.

His face filled with apprehension as he saw Jude come into the room. Jude was going to raise pure hell when he saw the fresh bottle before Deke.

"Jude's coming," Dent hissed.

Briscoe wasn't too drunk not to show concern, but it was too late to hide the bottle. Jude already was standing at the table.

He's seen the bottle all right, Dent thought. But he's got something else on his mind; something too big for him even to think about the bottle.

"I just saw Cal Decker," Jude announced abruptly. His eyes burned.

"Where?" Dent asked. He could appreciate Jude's hatred of Cal. Cal had kicked Jude full in the face, and it was a couple of weeks before Jude could talk well enough to make himself understood.

"I was just off work," Jude said breathlessly. "When I saw him coming down the other side of the street."

"You didn't do anything about it?" Dent asked disappointedly.

"He was armed," Jude snarled. "I wasn't."

That cunning look was back in Briscoe's eyes. He wasn't too drunk not to appreciate what Jude was saying. "Did you see where he went?"

"He went into Hale's office. I stood outside and watched for a long time," Jude replied.

"You think he's still there," Briscoe asked.

"He was when I left just a couple of minutes ago," Jude snapped.

Briscoe closed his hand into a tight, dirty fist and banged it on the table. "Both of them," he crowed. "In one grab." His eyes were scornful as he looked at the blank faces of his sons. "Goddammit, don't you see? What could hurt Pardee more than to lose both of his sons? That would crush that old bastard."

They still didn't get it, and Briscoe's face flushed with impassioned color. "We'll be waiting outside when they come out. I'll be across the street, and you two cover that office door from either side.

When they come out, we'll cut them down." He crackled with delight, as he watched their eyes start to burn. They got it now.

Briscoe stood and said, "Let's go get our rifles and be ready. He started off, then checked himself long enough to grab the bottle from the table. This would come in handy after Cal and Hale were cut down. They would need it for a celebration.

Chapter Twenty-two

HALE WHIPPED OUT the match and drew a lungful of smoke as he lifted his head. He didn't have time to say anything. The report of a rifle was obscenely loud. Hale threw his hands up to his head, reeled, then fell, sprawling out on the ground.

Cal stared at him, horror stricken. Before he could make a move toward Hale, another rifle barked, and Cal felt the bullet pluck at his sleeve. That came from a different direction than the first shot.

The second shot jolted Cal into action, and he dove from his feet, rolling as he hit the ground. My God, he was caught in a crossfire, for shots came from up and down the street and from across it. His numbed mind realized that at least three riflemen were shooting at him.

Cal grabbed for his pistol as he rolled, fighting his hampering coat to get at it. Some of those shots came too close. Geysers of dirt spewed up just behind him.

He wound up behind the post of a hitching rack. It was poor protection, but it was the best he could do. His lungs burned, and he gasped for breath as he tried to squeeze a big body behind the narrow width of a post. But he was thinking, and his eyes were alert and questing. Flame lanced at him from across the street. That located one of them. He ignored the other ambushers, concentrating on this one. He couldn't do any good by spewing his fire wildly at all three of them.

Cal waited until another burst of flame further located the one across the street. He could pick out the man now, an indistinct dark blob. He would say the figure was crouched or kneeling. Cal squeezed the trigger, and the dark form rose, growing taller and taller. Shrill screams rose from the figure before they broke off on a gurgling moan. The figure collapsed suddenly, and as it fell to the ground, Cal imagined he heard its thud.

"My God," a voice cried. "He's got Pa."

The crossfire increased in volume, and all around Cal, the ground heaved up in little vicious searching spouts. Cal felt a slug rip across the back of his leg, and he ground his teeth at the sharp stinging there.

He slewed around on the ground and located another of the bushwhackers. A dark form had stepped out from the shelter of a doorway, and the man must be levering shells into the chamber as fast as he could, for the spurts of flame looked like one constant stream of fire.

Cal aimed for the middle of that dark mass and shot. He was sure he had missed, for the figure didn't go down.

Before Cal could fire again, a brutal force slammed into his left shoulder. He almost dropped his pistol and struggled to hang onto the gun. He fought his numbed fingers, willing them to respond. He felt no pain, that spreading numbness. The pain would come later.

His eyes watered, and he fought desperately to concentrate. At times, there were two figures, then their hazy outlines blended into a single one.

Cal fired again. He heard the grunt as the man was slammed into a wall. The arms rose, throwing a weapon from him, then he fell. The rifle hit the ground several feet from the falling figure. The man lit in a sitting position, hung there for a long moment, then slowly toppled over.

It wasn't over yet, there was another left. It took laborious effort for Cal to force his muscles to obey his commands.

He sobbed and groaned as he slowly twisted around. Every instinct screamed for speed, but his muscles were too sluggish. Each movement set his shoulder to throbbing. He didn't know his face was bathed in sweat, his lips drawn back in a ghastly grimace. All he could hear was a great roaring noise, and his eyes refused to focus.

He thought he heard a thin, reedy voice screaming at the edge of the roaring, "Goddamn you. You killed Dent."

That was too much for Cal to reason through. He had a new problem. Did he hear the pound of running feet and were they heading toward or away from him? His mind was so tired. Those sounds of running feet had to be coming toward him and he vaguely heard additional firing.

A shot threw dirt up into Cal's face, and he blinked to clear his eyes. Another brutal force slammed into his side, and his mouth was open as he gasped. This time, he knew he couldn't hold onto the gun, but he couldn't believe it when he found it still in his hand. His eyes cleared enough so that he could see a dark mass rushing at him. My

God, the gun he held was such a tremendous weight. He struggled to raise it, and the muzzle kept wavering. He knew this was the best he could do, and he pulled the trigger once, then again. He couldn't tell how effective the shots were, and the hand was too weary to hold the gun any longer. The hovering blackness that had been hanging around the edges, strengthened and rushed in on him. Cal just let go, and welcomed the release it brought.

For several minutes, Cal had been aware of muted voices. He didn't want to open his eyes, for that would bring light, and light would unleash all the pain that he knew was waiting to grab him.

He tried to turn his head from the sounds, and that tiny movement released the pain. He tried to curse, and the oath came out as a garbled sound.

"Ah, he's coming to," a voice said, heavy with satisfaction. "I told you he would. He's too tough to let a few bullets stop him. Hey, Cal," the voice persisted. "Open your eyes."

Cal opened his eyes, then quickly closed them against the savage slash of light. He knew that would happen. Who in the hell was giving him such poor advice?

"Didn't I tell you so?" Now, the voice was triumphant. "Cal, look at me."

Cal opened his eyes again and blinked several times against the battering of the light. For a moment, panic seized him. He couldn't see; he was blind.

Cal fought off the welling panic. He couldn't be blind. He could see light and against it; he could make out the indefinite wavering lines of a man, standing near him.

Cal forced himself to stare until the wavering lines solidified. His eyes weren't bad; he could see the thick, dumpy form plainly.

"Hello, Doc," Cal said weakly.

Mathews blew out a long, relieved sigh. "You caused me some trouble, not to say anything about the worry," he said severely, but he was smiling. "You were shot to pieces. I had to take three bullets out of you."

As the bewilderment grew on Cal's face Mathews asked, "Don't you remember what happened?"

Cal started to shake his head, then stopped the gesture. Memory was coming back a small piece at a time. Those pieces grew and joined, and he had the whole picture; the flames spitting at him, the heavy reports of gunfire, the hard jolts when a bullet hit him.

"I was in a gun fight," he said. "I guess I blacked out."

Mathews snorted. "Blacked out? You've been unconscious for almost two days."

Cal's pulses picked up a hard beat of excitement as the missing details came back to him. "There were three of them," he said. "I remember that last one rushing me. Did I hit him?"

"Did you hit him?" Mathews echoed. "Dead center. You killed all three of them."

"My God," Cal said in a small, wondering voice. "Who were they?"

Mathews looked at him in amazement. "You didn't know? The Briscoes. Father and sons."

Cal remembered a voice screaming, "He shot Pa," then a little later another voice yelled, "You killed Dent."

"Oh, my God," Cal cried as the last detail fell into place, completing the picture. This was the most important detail of all, and he hadn't thought of it until this instant.

He tried to sit up, and Mathews pushed him back with a firm hand. "What are you trying to do, open up those wounds."

"They shot Hale," Cal said wildly.

Mathews turned his head. "Hale, you better move where he can see you, or I don't know what this wild man will do."

Hale stepped into Cal's view, and his arm was around Ellie. His head was swathed in bandages, but he was grinning broadly.

"Just a crease," Hale assured Cal. "But Doc told me I was lucky to have such a hard head." He chuckled, enjoying himself. "The Briscoes made a mistake. They should have known they couldn't hurt a Decker by shooting him in the head." His face sobered. "I won't try to say my thanks, Cal," he said gruffly. "When I came to, I thought you were dead." He shuddered at the memory. "By then, a lot of people were on the scene. Ellie was there, too. She insisted both of us be carried to the hotel. I couldn't get her to leave this room."

The lack of sleep showed in Ellie's drawn face, but Cal had never seen her look more radiant. For a moment, that lost little hope sprang to life in Cal, then he realized that shining look wasn't for him. Oh, she was grateful that he was alive, but the radiance was for Hale.

Cal's eyes were stinging as the hope died. It wasn't because of the dead hope, it was because Hale was alive.

Ellie left Hale's arm and approached Cal. She bent over him and whispered, "Do I have to tell you how thankful I am?"

"Phshaw, I didn't do anything special." Cal's grin was steady and true.

She bent and kissed him on the cheek, and Cal felt the quivering in her lips. When she raised her head, her eyes were shining through her tears. "You're an awful liar," she said. "But I'll forgive you for that one fault."

A voice yelled from outside the door, "Dammit, keep your paws off me. Nobody's keeping me from seeing my son."

Cal and Hale exchanged glances. There was no doubt whose voice that was. Pardee was here.

"Let me check with the doctor first and see if it's all right," Hobart said. The worry was pronounced in his voice.

"I don't need any damned doctor to tell me if I can see my son," Pardee boomed. "Mister, you'd better step out of the way."

Evidently, Hobart complied, for the door was flung open, and Pardee strode into the room. All his attention was on Cal, but Cal knew Pardee saw Hale, for his jawline tightened. Pardee never acknowledged Hale's presence in any way.

Pardee was better, Cal thought. Maybe it was the worry over him that had jolted Pardee out of his lethargy. Whatever it was, Cal was grateful for it.

Pardee stood over Cal, and his face was thunder

black. "Who did this? By God, I'll—"

That almost made Cal grin. That was the old Pardee.

Mathews interrupted Pardee. "Mr. Decker, your son has been badly wounded. There's no sense in agitating him further."

Pardee turned his head and glared at Mathews.

Mathews didn't flinch before those fierce, old eyes. "There's no use getting yourself and Cal all upset. It's over with. The Briscoes tried to waylay him." He nodded with satisfaction at Pardee's sagging jaw. "Yes, all three of them."

Cal saw the self-accusation flood Pardee's eyes. Pardee was blaming himself for this; for keeping the Briscoes on far too long.

"I'm sorry, son," Pardee mumbled.

Cal grinned. That was one of the rare apologies he had ever heard Pardee make. "Forget it, Pa," he said. "It's all over."

"You hurt bad?" Pardee demanded fiercely.

Mathews stepped in, incurring Pardee's further displeasure. "He's been hurt bad enough, Mr. Decker," He said crisply. "I took three bullets out of him."

A sweep of anguish twisted Pardee's features. His suffering was showing. "But he's all right?" he asked. "How long will he be laid up?"

Mathews shrugged. "That depends on him. In a month, maybe a little longer, he should be hobbling around. But he's going to have to take it easy for a while."

"Pa," Cal said. "Hale's here. The Briscoes shot him, too."

Pardee flicked his eyes at Hale. His lips tighted, and he never said a word.

Cal stared at his father in outrage afraid that no matter what happened, Pardee would carry his hardheadedness to the bitter end.

"Doc," Cal said, struggling up onto an elbow despite the pain it caused him. "I had some papers in my shirt pocket. Is that shirt still around here?"

At Mathews' puzzled nod, Cal said, "Get that shirt for me." He was beginning to boil. He'd be damned if he'd have this display of childishness any longer.

Mathews handed him the shirt, and Cal pulled the folded papers from the pocket and handed them to Pardee. "Read them," he said grimly.

Pardee stared at the papers, his eyes growing ever wider. He looked at Cal, his confusion apparent. "These are bills of sale. Hell, I never bought any cattle."

"No," Cal agreed. He managed to keep from shouting at Pardee. "But Hale did." Cal ignored the frantic gestures Hale was making at him. Everything was going to be out in the open now. "Three thousand head to replace the cows you lost. He's trying to put you back on your feet. Goddammit, he is your son. And you treat him like dirt."

Pardee's face turned a mottled red and white. "He ain't my son," he squalled. "I didn't ask him to do this, did I?"

Cal didn't have time to pour out the heated words that were crowding up into his mouth, because Ellie didn't give him the chance.

She walked toward Pardee and thrust her face close to his. "Mr. Decker, I was prepared to like you because you are Hale's father. I see that I wa[s] wrong. You are an unforgiving, hardheaded ol[d] man."

Pardee blinked several times at the ferocity o[f] her onslaught. "Who do you think you are, to tal[k] to me like this?" he blustered.

Hale was trying to quiet Ellie with a singula[r] lack of success.

She was really worked up. Her eyes snapped and she breathed hard. "I know what happene[d] between you two," she rushed on. "You slappe[d] Hale, and he knocked you down. It was unpardon[-]able between a father and son. Hale inherite[d] much of your hardheadedness, but there's hope fo[r] him. He's young enough to see where he wa[s] wrong. He tried to make it up, but you wouldn'[t] have it. There's no hope at all for a stubborn, ol[d] man." She blinked angrily at the tears that kep[t] welling into her eyes.

"Nobody has to give me anything," Parde[e] said, but the bluster was gone out of his voice.

All of a sudden, he seemed to collapse inwardly[.] He looked at Hale and asked plaintively, "Who i[s] she?"

Hale tried to keep his face straight, but the twitching lip corners threatened to betray him[.] "She's going to be your new daughter-in-law."

"Oh, my God," Pardee said in anguish. H[e] glared at Hale. "Do you know what you're gettin[g] into."

"I do," Hale said gravely.

"She's going to put a ring in your nose and yank on it every time she thinks you're getting out o[f] line."

"I'm looking forward to it," Hale said promptly.

Cal stared in disbelief. Hale and Pardee were talking together almost amiably.

"Never saw a redheaded filly that wasn't a handful of trouble," Pardee grumbled. He gulped several times, then said, "I hope you know what you're doing."

"I do," Hale replied.

Cal watched Pardee try to say something and knew how hard it was for him. Pardee was always an awkward man with words.

"About those cattle, Hale. I guess I'll keep them. Too much trouble getting them back where they belong." Then the old fierceness came back into his face. "But I'm telling you one thing. A third of them belongs to you." At the growing disagreement in Hale's face, he roared, "Do you want to be a part of this family or not?"

"Anything you say, Pa," Hale said meekly.

That damned Hale, Cal thought. Everything he touches turns out right for him. Ellie was smiling, and Cal had never seen anything so beautiful.

Pardee whirled on her. "As for you, young lady. If you're going to be part of this family, you're going to have to learn respect for your father-in-law."

Ellie moved over to Pardee and slipped her hand under his arm. "Yes, sir," she said. "Anything you say, father."

Pardee was grinning all over his face. "Reminds me of your mother, Cal. The hair's a different color, but the spirit is the same. I never dared talk back to her much, either."

"What are you grinning about?" Pardee roared. "If you think you're going to lie around on your ass when there's so much work to do, you've got another think coming."

Nothing could remove that grin from Cal's face. Mathews was a good enough doctor all right, but Cal was going to prove how wrong Mathews was in his estimate of the recovery period. Hell, he'd bet right now that he'd beat that time by a good two weeks.

There are a lot more where this one came from!

ORDER your FREE catalog of ACE paperbacks here. We have hundreds of inexpensive books where this one came from priced from 75¢ to $2.50. Now you can read all the books you have always wanted to at tremendous savings. Order your *free* catalog of ACE paperbacks now.

CE BOOKS ● Box 576, Times Square Station ● New York, N.Y. 10036

The MS READ-a-thon needs young readers!

Boys and girls between 6 and 14 can join the MS READ-a-thon and help find a cure for Multiple Sclerosis by reading books. And they get two rewards — the enjoyment of reading, and the great feeling that comes from helping others.

Parents and educators: For complete information call your local MS chapter, or call toll-free (800) 243-6000. Or mail the coupon below.

Kids can help, too!

Mail to:
National Multiple Sclerosis Society
205 East 42nd Street
New York, N.Y. 10017

I would like more information about the MS READ-a-thon and how it can work in my area.

MS Mystery Sleuth

Name _____
(please print)
Address _____
City _____ State ____ Zip ____
Organization _____

MS-ACE